A Sinister Assassin

T0017398

ANTONIN ARTAUD

A SINISTER ASSASSIN

IVRY-SUR-SEINE,

SEPTEMBER 1947 TO MARCH 1948

EDITED, TRANSLATED AND
WITH AN INTRODUCTION BY
STEPHEN BARBER

DIAPHANES

This book is in loving memory of
Pierre Guyotat (1940–2020)

Stephen Barber

Introduction

Antonin Artaud's very last work, prior to his death in March 1948, is the most extraordinary element of his entire body of work – and is the element now most enduringly inspirational, for contemporary artists, filmmakers, musicians, writers, choreographers, and others inspired by Artaud – through its fiercely exploratory, extreme and combative forms, along with its dissolutions and negations of forms, focused above all on the human anatomy, as well as on sonic experimentation and on provocations for innovation in dance and performance. This book assembles Artaud's crucial work from September 1947 to March 1948, when that work was concentrated spatially into its location at his pavilion in the grounds of a convalescence clinic in Ivry-sur-Seine, on the southern edge of Paris – and especially on the insurgent, fragmentary work of the final weeks of his life.

The now-vanished two-room eighteenth-century pavilion, where Artaud spent the final part of his life, was located within the clinic's extensive and heavily-wooded parkland. At the same time, it held an urban location, positioned directly against a high street-wall at the southern edge of the clinic's grounds, directly across the rue de la Mairie (now the avenue Georges Grosnat) from Ivry-sur-Seine's town-hall, as is evident from a series of photographs of the pavilion taken by Artaud's close collaborator Paule Thévenin and her brother Georges Pastier, in which the pavilion appears an abandoned, lost-in-time edifice, its exterior walls decayed and decrepit. Of the pavilion's two rooms, only one was used by Artaud; as documented in photographs by Denise Colomb, it held a wooden bed pushed close to the large ornate fireplace, an armchair, and a side-table piled with notebooks, manuscripts and empty bottles, directly alongside two blocks of wood which Artaud hammered and hacked while writing and reading-aloud his work. The main room's walls held Artaud's own drawings, either pinned into them, or else enclosed in glass frames propped against the base of the walls.

Artaud's pavilion, together with the entirety of the clinic's expanse of many buildings, were demolished over the years following his death there, generating a vast wasteland. After its improvised use for Ivry-sur-Seine's markets and fairs, that emptied-out terrain eventually came to form two public parks, the northern part incorporated into what is now the Parc des Cornailles and the southern part – the site of Artaud's pavilion – transformed into the far smaller Parc Maurice Thorez, flanked by high-rise municipal apartment blocks constructed in 1953.

The Ivry-sur-Seine clinic was, by 1948, a largely unregulated private establishment; it had originated in the 1820s, and was successively named after each of its directors. Usually, those directors were maverick doctors who had not been able to habituate themselves to working within state institutions, though in the preceding years of warfare and German Occupation, even institutionally ill-attuned doctors with anarchistic or anti-authoritarian beliefs, such as Gaston Ferdière – a former Surrealist poet preoccupied with pornography and fetishism, who had run the Rodez asylum during Artaud's years there – had recast themselves as figures of social power in charge of state institutions. The Ivry-sur-Seine convalescence clinic was owned and run when Artaud arrived there by Dr François Achille-Delmas, a proto anti-psychiatrist and specialist on paralysis and suicide, who treated Artaud with indulgence but died suddenly in 1947 during Artaud's time at his clinic. That great indulgence of Achille-Delmas along with his erratic therapeutic approach is evident in a journal entry of Artaud's young friend Jacques Prevel from 20 May 1947, in which Artaud informs Prevel: 'My testicles were suppurating all through the night with a profuse, blackish pus. Dr Delmas said to me: "That's beyond my expertise", and he added: "You're going to need to have a gramme of heroin every day."'[1] The convalescence clinic charged fees for Artaud's 22-months-long stay there, paid from funds (administered by a lawyer) that were raised by his friends both before and after his release from his forcible incarceration of 1943–46 at the asylum of Rodez; Rodez, in rural southern France, where Artaud was given electro-convulsive treatment, had been the last of the asylums in which he spent nine years following his apocalyptic journey to Ireland in 1937. Those funds also paid for Artaud's day-to-day living costs; he was destitute on his release from Rodez, and made almost no money at all from his writings, drawings and radio projects of 1946–48.

Most Parisians in 1948 (and now) would have considered Ivry-sur-Seine as a grim zonal area to be avoided at all costs, and the very last place on earth they would want to end up in. Most people chose to live there either because of its left-wing aura or because it was very inexpensive. Twenty years later, the prominent Artaud-inspired writer Pierre Guyotat spent the winter of 1968–69 in the parallel suburb located immediately to the south of Ivry-sur-Seine – Vitry-sur-Seine – sharing a low-cost tower-block apartment with several friends, and wrote one of his best-known books, *Eden, Eden, Eden*, while living there, but returned to central Paris as soon as he could afford to. Despite Ivry-sur-Seine's reputation in Artaud's time there as a dire and polluted hellhole, he clearly appreciated his pavilion, with its relative solitude, after his nine years of asylum incarceration spent in the incessant cacophony of crowded communal wards.

Ivry-sur-Seine was Artaud's terminal location, situated at the end of the métro line from central Paris which had only opened three weeks before Artaud moved there, as though the line's extension to its last station, Mairie d'Ivry – situated close to the clinic's entry gates – had been constructed specially to facilitate Artaud's journeys into central Paris. In post-war Paris, the city's electricity supply remained erratic, and métro journeys were often still subject in 1948 to frequent power-cuts, with métro passengers sitting in darkness in tunnels for long spans of time before the current could be reactivated. Ivry-sur-Seine had been a thriving port-suburb of Paris in the nineteenth century, with many riverside warehouses; by 1948, it was still enduring the last phase of its already-lengthy industrial decline. Its population was overwhelmingly left-wing, with a Communist mayor in 1948; its citizens had departed in great numbers a decade or so earlier to fight in the Spanish Civil War. Artaud's final location in Ivry-sur-Seine came about entirely by chance, after his friend Arthur Adamov, who negotiated Artaud's release from Rodez, asked Paule Thévenin, a former medical student with time to spare for the task, to search out an inexpensive convalescence home, close to Paris, in which Artaud could have total freedom of movement. She began that search – before having met Artaud – from her home in Charenton, close to Ivry-sur-Seine; Dr Achille-Delmas was one of the first doctors with whom she discussed accommodating Artaud on his release from Rodez.

Artaud arrived there on 27 May 1946, and soon afterwards requested permission from Dr Achille-Delmas to move from his assigned room in one of the clinic's main buildings to a small pavilion that he had seen while walking in the grounds. It was one of the many abandoned pavilions scattered around the gardens; Artaud's chosen pavilion was close to the clinic's main gate, and was located next to a much larger pavilion that was also abandoned. Dr Achille-Delmas agreed, and arranged for Artaud's rudimentary meals to be carried out to him, and for one of the gardeners to bring wood for the pavilion's fireplace.

Artaud made daily journeys into Paris for the first sixteen or so months that he lived in Ivry-sur-Seine, visiting friends from the 1930s years before his incarceration and writing in cafes, often in the company of the tubercular poet, Jacques Prevel, who barely outlasted Artaud and died in 1951. But from around September 1947, Artaud was often ill and made far fewer journeys into Paris, thereby accentuating his inhabitation of his Ivry-sur-Seine pavilion and its pre-eminent location for his work. His newer, younger friends visited him often at his pavilion. The onset of Artaud's ailing condition coincided with that of Prevel, who was hospitalised from the autumn of 1947 and could no longer spend his days scouring Paris for laudanum, heroin, morphine and chloral hydrate to take to Artaud in Ivry-sur-Seine. As a result, Artaud now had to find his own drugs, and when he did go into central Paris, it was often for a journey with dual aims, involving travelling northwards to Montmartre to acquire drugs from that district's many street-dealers, along with visits southwards to friends and publishers in Saint-Germain-des-Prés and Montparnasse. An example of those urban journeys is marked in Artaud's furious, rapidly-written final letter to one of his publishers, Pierre Bordas, from 14 February 1948, sent the day after he had appeared at the publisher's office in Montparnasse in wild disarray after visiting drug-dealers in Montmartre, and had been brusquely turned away by the receptionist: 'Sir, I'm very ill, so ill that when I had a consultation with Prof. Mondor at the Salpêtrière hospital, I was forbidden to leave my bed for several months. So, I can almost never come into Paris. Yesterday, 13 February, I wanted to take advantage of a *very rare* journey into Paris to come and see you... but my name is Antonin Artaud and you have published one of my books entitled *Artaud the Mômo* which has just sold out in the space of several days... you have made a killing with *Artaud the Mômo* picked up a fortune all that *stinks*...'.[2] Artaud's drug-dealers sometimes also became his Ivry-sur-Seine pavilion visitors, travelling southwards across the entire city to threaten him when his debts accumulated; such journeys proved futile, as Artaud reported to Prevel: 'One of them came to see me, one from Montmartre, but he soon gave up. I told him: look, I've only got 20 francs left. With me, he soon realised that he had to give up, that I've gone too far, too far by a very long way, when it comes to drugs.'[3] Artaud also made frequent journeys eastwards in his last months, from the Ivry-sur-Seine clinic by foot or via a local bus across the bridge over the river Seine for the short distance to the adjacent district of Charenton and to the apartment where Paule Thévenin lived with her daughter Domnine and her husband, Yves, a doctor; Artaud made that journey for the last time on the day preceding the night of his death.

Artaud was due to vacate the Ivry-sur-Seine pavilion on 15 March 1948. Its new director, Dr Georges Rallu, who had taken over the clinic following the death of Dr Achille-Delmas, was less inclined to be indulgent towards Artaud, so making it a far less conducive site for him; Dr Rallu also had plans to close down the clinic, which Artaud's visitors often perceived as being in a state of terminal dilapidation. Artaud envisaged travelling from Ivry-sur-Seine to Antibes on the Mediterranean coast for the rest of the winter, to continue his post-asylum convalescence in a villa whose rental costs had been paid in advance; even so, he appears to have been ambivalent about making that journey.

In the last months of his life, Artaud appeared ancient, toothless and emaciated, though he was only 51 years old and his new friends, such as Paule Thévenin, perceived him as a still-young man, enduringly holding the residues of the startling facial beauty he had as a film actor twenty years earlier; he worked incessantly, and was able to out-distance anyone with his fast walking pace. Artaud appears to have been ill at the end of his life, either with intestinal or rectal cancer. He unequivocally told the *Combat* journalist Jean Marabini, in their interview a week before his death: 'I know I have cancer'. The specialist Professor Mondor told Artaud at their consultation at Paris's Salpêtrière hospital on 6 February 1948 that he had severe intestinal infections and needed rest; Mondor may have wanted to avoid giving Artaud a diagnosis of late-stage cancer. By contrast, Gaston Ferdière, Artaud's doctor at the Rodez asylum, told me – perhaps implausibly – that he believed Artaud had no cancer at all (since he would have been able to identify it himself at Rodez in 1946), and that, in examining Artaud, Mondor must have mistaken compacted intestinal residues of long-term drug abuse for cancerous formations. In any case, no specific programme of treatment was proposed for Artaud, even if he had allowed it. His letters of his last weeks indicate that he was experiencing blackouts and haemorrhages at his pavilion. In a letter from Ivry-sur-Seine to another of his publishers, Marc Barbezat, on 16 February 1948, he writes that he has 'just had 3 attacks here and I was found *bathing* in my blood,/a great pool of blood...'.[4] Artaud appears to have died from an overdose of chloral hydrate; it's uncertain if the dose he drank was intentional, and it probably was not. A lethal dose of chloral hydrate is variable and unpredictable; Artaud never regulated his intake, often taking very large nocturnal doses, as he confided to Prevel, and he could very easily have died on numerous previous occasions. Artaud's approach to drugs was always to have the absolute maximum amount available to him at all times; often, in his notebooks, he demands the immediate delivery to him of drugs in quantities of many 'tons', and he continued in February 1948 to travel to Montmartre to acquire drugs from illicit dealers even after Mondor had given him a prescription authorising him to have an unlimited 'official' supply of opium.

It was unusually cold in the Paris region around the end of February 1948, with snowstorms. On Artaud's last night, 3–4 March, Ivry-sur-Seine was still frozen, with snow on the ground. Artaud appears to have died suddenly while getting dressed in the middle of the night, and was found in the morning with a shoe in his hand, stretched-out on the floor of the pavilion's main room. He was initially buried in the local municipal cemetery of Ivry-sur-Seine, a short distance from his pavilion, wearing an old blue overcoat donated by a friend and with a bunch of violets placed between his fingers, but was disinterred in 1975, his bones mechanically crushed into fragments by a funeral company so that they could be transported in a small box, and moved from Ivry-sur-Seine to the Artaud family grave in Marseille's St Pierre cemetery; in 2023, he remains there.

*

The time of these writings of Artaud's last months was marked especially by the furore in the first days of February 1948 over the censorship placed on his radio broadcast, *To have done with the judgement of god*; the bitter ending to that broadcast's planned transmission led directly to the visits to Artaud's Ivry-sur-Seine pavilion of the two newspaper journalists who (especially in Jean Marabini's interview) give vivid accounts of Artaud's inhabitation of that location in the last week of his life, though Artaud, preoccupied with death, barely speaks about the broadcast's censorship in either interview. Artaud had been wounded especially by the contempt with which France's national radio station, having first commissioned the project, then banned it, with disdain, 'exactly as if it were a porno movie', as Paule Thévenin told me. The broadcast's envisioned reconfiguration of the human anatomy, in its new manifestation of corporeal apocalypse – initiated in zonal suburban Paris, after the global apocalypse foreseen in Artaud's 1937 Ireland letters written from Galway and from the outlandish, beyond-the-world terrain of Inishmore island – appeared for a time to have been literally erased, though the audio recording's re-emergence in the 1950s and 60s eventually led to the wide audience engagement to which Artaud had been deeply attached in 1948.

In his last months, as throughout the final three years of his life, Artaud's main medium for his writings took the form of notebooks – inexpensively manufactured notebooks intended for use by schoolchildren – which he always carried, folded, often several at a time, in his coat-pockets. His very last notebook – the 406th since he began using them at the asylum of Rodez – seizes Artaud's death in its sudden mid-page arrest on the night of 3–4 March 1948. In addition to that notebook medium – used for drawings, and amalgams of drawings with writings, as well as for writings – Artaud also dictated his texts whenever he could, and wrote too on loose sheets of ochre-coloured paper, as with his many letters. In his Ivry-sur-Seine pavilion, he also made larger-scale drawings, often pinning pieces of thick paper to his room's walls before assailing them with pencils and crayons while standing upright, or else working in his armchair if he were making a facial portrait of a visitor to his pavilion. Alongside his work in his final months on his drawings – including the completion of the drawing *The Projection of the true body* – he also wrote the last of his texts about his own drawings (after two previous texts from 1947) on 31 January 1948, for his unrealized book project intended to assemble a large selection of his notebook drawings, *50 Drawings to assassinate magic*.

In Artaud's notebooks, to their very last words, he amasses incantations and denunciations of malevolent, proliferating figures – sinister agents of societal power – who are now aiming, after many previous thwarted attempts and via covert magical manoeuvres, to infiltrate his pavilion to steal his semen and ultimately to assassinate him, as he believed had happened to many other insurgent poets and artists before him. On his last night, he is lucidly alert, upright, on guard *in extremis* to the point of hallucination, wide-awake, at the moment of death.

*

These translations of Artaud's final writings were undertaken directly from the original handwritten manuscript notebooks and letters, from an original copy of the special issue from June 1948 of the arts magazine *84*, and from original issues of the newspapers in which Artaud's final interviews appeared. For their support and warm encouragement, I am grateful especially to Guillaume Fau and Laurence Engel at the Bibliothèque nationale de France in Paris, where most of Artaud's manuscripts are kept, to Albert Dichy at the IMEC research centre near Caen, Normandy, to Edmund White, to Pierre Guyotat, with whom I discussed this project at our last meeting before his death in 2020, and to Sylvère Lotringer and Clayton Eshleman, who both died in 2020–21.

My aim with that approach, however obstinate, has been to avoid the subsequent institutional 'collected' editions of Artaud's writings (both those of Paule Thévenin and, subsequently, of Évelyne Grossman, the latter of which contests the former) and to maintain, as far as possible, a tangible connection with the rawness of the live moment in which Artaud was working at his Ivry-sur-Seine pavilion in the winter of 1947–48. This assembling of Artaud's last writings attempts to keep at a distance those potentially ossifying and institutionalising editions that accumulated over the seven decades after Artaud's death, becoming increasingly fraught with rancour and feuds that have nothing to do with Artaud's work. Artaud himself refused the connection between death and institutionalisation, writing in February 1947: 'to die, that's to pass into the realm of being/enter into the system of the institution'.[5] By contrast, this book's aim – even if it's an impossible one – is to create a fragmented, disintegrated edition of Artaud's most intensive and corporeally interrogative work, in its expansiveness, as it accelerated into and against death in his life's final months.

This book draws too from my meetings and interviews across the second half of the 1980s in Paris with many of the figures Artaud worked with, and whom he invokes in these writings. Those figures had all been in their twenties or thirties at the time of their encounters with Artaud, but by then were nearing the ends of their lives: Paule Thévenin, laughing wryly but wrung-out by forty years of editing Artaud's work, as she showed me his drawings arranged around all of the walls of her Paris apartment, part of a former factory; the Rodez asylum director Gaston Ferdière in his office at a private clinic in the district of Aubervilliers (a decrepit northern-Paris suburban equivalent to Ivry-sur-Seine) with his liquid-spattered white doctor's coat, having – as he told me – just electroshocked a child; Marc Barbezat, at his palatial apartment on Paris's Île Saint-Louis overlooking the Seine and the Institut du Monde Arabe, remembering Artaud's guileless attempts to cheat him over the *Tutuguri* variants,

Marcel Bisiaux, Chris Marker, and others. Older figures mentioned in these writings, or relevant to them, such as Jean Paulhan, Pierre Loeb, and Roger Blin, had died already by then. The idea for a book assembling Artaud's very last writings emerged at the end of those years in Paris, in 1990, but it has taken another thirty years for it to happen.

This book is in seven parts. From the texts in their entirety drawn from the special issue of the magazine *84*, there follow Artaud's two major texts from his life's final month or so – *50 Drawings to assassinate magic*, from 31 January 1948, and *Tutuguri*, from 16 February 1948 – then seven letters from Artaud's final period, followed by his two newspaper interviews of his life's last week, with *Combat* and *Le Figaro Littéraire*, then the fragmentary texts of his final notebook of the first days of March 1948, and ending with the glossolalia inscribed around one of his last-finished drawings, *The Projection of the true body*.

NOTES

1 Jacques Prevel, *En compagnie d'Antonin Artaud* (Paris: Flammarion, 1994), p. 162.

2 Antonin Artaud, letter to Pierre Bordas, 14 February 1948 (collection of the Bibliothèque nationale de France, Paris).

3 *En compagnie d'Antonin Artaud*, p. 161.

4 Antonin Artaud, letter to Marc Barbezat, 16 February 1948, *l'arve et l'aume suivi de 24 lettres à Marc Barbezat* (Décines: L'Arbalète, 1989), p. 96.

5 Notes pour une 'Lettre aux Balinais', *Tel Quel*, Issue 46, Summer 1971, p. 32.

ANTONIN ARTAUD

antonin artaud

84

FINAL FRAGMENTS

ARTAUD'S LAST WRITINGS FROM SEPTEMBER 1947
TO FEBRUARY 1948, PUBLISHED IN THE MAGAZINE
84, ISSUE 5/6, JUNE 1948

On Artaud's death in March 1948, his friends decided to publish his last writings as a special double issue, numbered 5/6, of the small-scale literary magazine *84*, run by a group of young poets headed by Marcel Bisiaux; Artaud had published his work in previous issues of *84* and the magazine's cover used an element of one of his drawings. The title *84* came from the street-number of Bisiaux's apartment on the Île St Louis in Paris. The magazine, intended primarily for young readers, lasted for a further three years, until 1951, and its closure was marked on 27 May 1951 with a broadcast in the French national radio station's experimental 'Club d'essai' series, including excerpts from recordings by Artaud and Roger Blin, in which *84*'s young editors discussed its aims, excitedly talking over one another. Bisiaux became a journalist and wrote a book on writers' cats.

The special issue's printing appears to have been funded with Artaud's own remaining money at his death, collected from his pavilion and his coat pockets (the equivalent of what would now be around £250–£300, according to Marcel Bisiaux and Paule Thévenin). It was printed inexpensively, on thin paper, with several pages devoted to advertisements for bookshops, publishers and art galleries, including the Galerie Pierre at which Artaud had exhibited his drawings in the previous year, 1947. The issue consists of 40 pages of mostly short, disconnected texts drawn from Artaud's notebooks and manuscripts of the period September 1947 to February 1948; a further 15 pages – not translated here – assembled memories and invocations of Artaud by his friends. Bisiaux (1922–1990) and Thévenin (1918–1993) jointly edited the texts as a rapidly assembled and personal selection; Thévenin was able to date them reliably since she had worked closely with Artaud throughout the past year and a half.

These texts, with their erratic punctuation, were translated directly from an original copy of *84*. The translation also draws indirectly from my interviews of 1985–90 with Thévenin and Bisiaux in Paris. Breaks between texts are indicated by asterisks.

Artaud's fragments form autonomous, aberrant entities, enforcing a distinctive separation between themselves and the engulfing, normalising language around them. In Artaud's hands, a fragment is a jagged and resistant instrument or weapon. Towards the end of the selected material, the fragments accumulate into a more and more abbreviated, honed and fierce configuration. Alongside the predominantly fragmentary texts, the *84* editors also included a letter from Artaud to Paule Thévenin, and an extended text from November 1947 that was originally intended to be recorded for the radio broadcast *To have done with the judgement of god*, but which had to be excluded from it due to the recording's time constraints: *The Theatre of Cruelty*.

These fragments exist in a torn-open editorial state, in intimacy with Artaud's death (and its profound shock for his friends), and directly manifesting it; the *84* magazine special issue literally came into existence through Artaud's death, embodying it. The texts form a rendering of Artaud's death, but they also appear askew: assembled haphazardly (as the editors freely admitted), without any great editorial experience and deploying an intentional and even defiant maladroitness, and driven by their editors' primary aim to collect what they believed Artaud would have most wanted to survive from his immediate work. The magazine also served as a vital restitution of Artaud's work, soon after his death; prior to his death, Artaud's most recent experience had been the brutal censoring of his work. The *84* magazine's special issue texts have never previously been republished in this form in any language, and they retain their own transmission of Artaud's infinite, inassimilable last combat.

Final Fragments,
from the magazine 84

Thoughts do not pass from one to the other
neither through sequencing nor through being
    welded together
and that's why it needs to be known
what it is that I want

whenever, thinking about a christian
it's instead the jew who appears
and why it is
I throw myself towards the jew in order to defend him
lovingly
while at the same time I'm fighting him

So, to whom am I going to deliver an account of my
    transgression?

to the curvature of the wing of this angel
or to some kind of shifting light
to some lost photophore
to some kind of gathering of stinking macaques
all of them armed with crosses
wielding enemas made from crosses

stinking too of dirty laundry, of incense,
of holy oils, etc...
breathing out argumentative drivel

from myself
  to myself
    who is it that comes
      and who is it that goes?

Has he been lying
or was there really at stake solely the thought of a
    god who was passing
living only from his own act of sacrilege.

So, they are living from their own act of sacrilege

from having sat down
from having shat on the body of god
from having invented shit with that body
from having extracted shit from that body!

All of us are enveloped by a secondary humanity
a humanity that is malevolent and sinister
which draws its roots from within the bodies of
    everyday human beings
who at certain moments
realise they have become vampires
and brutally start to act as vampires.
Those people are among the ones who didn't kill
    the beast in themselves as it was being born
they're the ones who refused to detach themselves
    from the beast
because they were too attached to it.
That beast is a bottomless eroticism,
arising from the grim day of an eroticism of the
    world's abysses
that you can discover, just by shutting your eyes.

It's there that you can see the hideous world of
    lubricity convulsing
without any hole, without any distinction
all of it striated by lubricity.

it's there that you can see emerge the obscene
    proposal
for a world without evaluation, nor morality
and that would be entirely occupied by evil.

It's there, that the beasts
– who are wedded to the entire spectrum
of an over-colourised, sinister passion –
are endlessly born,
each of them out of the other,
through gaps in the air,
through drifting emptinesses in space,
it's there, that sex unleashes its own laws
and liberates itself from the law,
you are not going to be able to see all this
unless you yourself exude and sweat-out a vile
    liquified atmosphere,
unless you weep from your anus and from your eyes,
unless you snort out an unidentifiable snot
which exudes from your nose as it does from your
    eyelids
which hurls out screams that are suffocated and
    beaten back as though being buried under the
    earth
screams from a swelling-up eczema suddenly dislo-
    cated from its state of ease.

November 1947.

*

The beings do not appear in the exterior day

The only power they have is to spurt out into the
    subterranean night where they do their work.

But, across the eternities
that they've passed their own time
and passed time itself
in that self-focused action,
not one of them has ever generated itself.

You'll have to wait until the hand of the Man seizes
    hold of them and works on them

because it's only
the Man
– inborn and predestined for that work –
who holds
that fearsome
and
ineffable
inborn
capability

Now bring out the body of the human being
into the light of nature
plunge that body, raw, into the glow of nature
that's where the sun will finally merge with it.

February 1948.

*

The body is the body
it's alone
and has no need of organs,
the body never is an organism
organisms are the enemies of the body
whatever things are created then go on all alone
    without the intervention of any organ
every organ is a parasite,
it covers up a parasitic mission
intended to enable the birth of a being which
    should never have existed there
Organs have only ever been made in order to give
    beings something to eat, while beings have been
    condemned in their very conception and have
    no reason to exist in the first place
Reality itself has not yet come into existence because
    the true organs of the human body have still not
    yet been created nor positioned into place.
The theatre of cruelty was created in order to complete
    that putting into place and to accomplish –

through a new dance of the human body – a
crushing of this world of microbes which is
nothing but a coagulated abyss.
The theatre of cruelty is intended to make eyelids
dance in intimacy with elbows, with kneecaps,
with femurs, and with toes and you are now
going to see all that

November 1947

*

I was alive
and I had been <u>there</u> for <u>all of time</u>
Had I been eating?

No
but when I was hungry, I recoiled, with my body,
and I didn't eat myself up
but all of that fell apart
some strange kind of intervention took place
I wasn't ill
I was in the act of reconquering health
always through the recoiling of my body backwards
my body betrayed me
it still didn't sufficiently know me
eating: that's to project forward what has to be kept
confined to the back

Was I sleeping?

No, I wasn't sleeping
you need to be chaste in order to know how not to
eat
If you open up our mouth, you're exposing yourself
to the miasmas.
So then, no mouth!
No mouth
no tongue

no teeth
no larynx
no esophagus
no stomach
no belly
no anus

I am going to reconstruct the man that I am

November 1947.

*

The location where you suffer from it
in which it is known that you are suffering
the location in which you feel it
and in which
systematically
and wilfully
the things that are created are maintained
those things that are eaten by it
at the heart of eternal pain
without ever pemitting those things to go and
    huddle up within an organ
– an always useless organ –
that's where a <u>being</u> is awaiting them

This is how it's certain that there is nothing more
heinously useless and superfluous than the organ
which is called the heart
which is the dirtiest medium that the beings were
ever able to invent to pump away at the life within
me.
The heart's movements are nothing other than a
manoeuvre by which the being is able ceaselessly
to perpetrate itself upon me in order to take away
from me that which I ceaselessly refuse to the
being,
that's to say: that with which it can survive

Beings are this virtual, parasitic life which created
itself at the margins of true life
and which has ended up by having the effrontery to
replace true life.
Our present life, considered in itself,
constitutes exactly one of those bifurcations created
by beings at the edges of real life
and which has ended up by forgetting that it's
falsified
and has ended up having the effrontery to observe
real life follow behind in the tracks of its heinous
movement

November 1947.

*

Ivry, 1 September 1947

Madame Paule Thévenin
dear Paule,

Telling you that I'm unhappy is really nothing and
a little word when I'm confronted with the hor-
rendous feeling of irrelevancy, of dissatisfaction, of
malaise, of rancour, of exasperation, of dishearted-
ness, of maladjustment of the heart, when faced
with certain circumstances.
I need to be able to find a particular quantity of
opium for each day – I really need it, because I have
a body that's been wounded in its bone-marrow's
nerves and that situation is now irrecoverable, incur-
able, absolutely irrecoverable. There's no surgical
operation that could return to me the nerves of an
organism which has lost them.
I've evaluated the minimum amount of opium
I need to be the equivalent of thirty grammes of
laudanum for each day.

You can't say that's at all excessive.
It's a scandal that I'm not able to procure for myself
even that small minimum amount.
I didn't have it at Rodez, at Ville Evrard, at Sainte-
Anne, at Rouen,
but my life there was that of a desperately ill para-
lytic who spent his days stretched out on his bed,
only ever getting up in a sudden, uncontrollable
movement to write or to draw, before returning to a
prone state a few minutes later.
In order to be able to travel to the ile de Ré, I would
need to gather together a supply – not just enough
to spend 15 days there but enough to hold myself
together long enough in order to endure a <u>detoxica-
tion</u>.
I'm sure that the sea air will keep me going and will
help me to resist certain states of need, but on the
condition that those states would not be <u>too cruel</u>
and too prolonged.
In any case, I can't even find a supply enough for 8
to 10 days out of the planned 15 to 20 days of the
stay there.
You've always had your health, so you know nothing
about what it is to have a body which is in need of an
<u>element</u> – you're absolutely incapable of visualising it,
of imagining what a body is that <u>lacks</u>
not what it needs in order to live
but what it needs to avoid the pain of enduring
having to be alive
when all of my teeth are as though proclaiming
their absence
at the heart of a
DECAY-RIDDEN
<u>nutritional</u>
gingivitus

I don't know if you're going to be able to under-
stand me.

But I see myself surrounded by bodies that are
sweating out life, that are bursting outward with
life – and which have never known what it is to
have an essential absence
an absence upon an essential point
of a security, of a support, of an assurance,
no: they know nothing at all of what it is to experi-
ence the slipping-away and the taking-flight of that
assurance
and which the intestines' ceaseless digestive game
undertaken beneath the jawbones' occult shadows
never rendered normal.
and what really constitutes life is always that absent
tooth caught within the other tooth's intestinal
mastication – that other work of dentition which is
enforced and ossified
because it's waiting:
what is it waiting for?
it's waiting for the unending, pierced-through
pain – which reveals the unstable and never-satis-
fied face of things –
to be made silent for a time and to stop speaking in
the face of
the great drainage,
the fathomless and borderless gushing-away of
what is no longer an opening out
and which is now concealed
when it can't anymore be made the squared or the
'<u>prolonged</u>'.

What I mean to say is that, for a certain kind of
pain, you need unknown remedies and that you are
not going to find those remedies anymore in the
field of medicine nor in corporeal anatomy,
but instead in anatomy that has been de-corpore-
alised.

I'm hoping to be able to COME to the ile de Ré.
I'll see you soon.

*

Being has innumerable states which are becoming
    more and more dangerous and about which
    people know nothing.
Non-being also has its states, and you could say that
    states and certain states supposedly of being
    could really belong to non-being – but you can
    get hold of being in its states, etc, etc…
AND WHAT HAVE YOU DONE WITH MY BODY, GOD?
that's exactly what every individual
who is able to question,
to interject, has the right to ask, now.

So, what exactly is god?
The consortium of the universal gathering-together
of all forms of slothfulnesses
and of all forms of cowardices
bought-up around the effort
of living solely as one body

God is that pea-seed made of the shrinking and
    lascivious matter of being
who really wants to give himself away
to let himself be taken
but who doesn't want himself to be seized.
To be touched, played around with,
rubbed up against, commingled with
– but not given away –
so there's always this idea
that there exists some kind of third force
or
    <u>element</u>
which is finally the sole originator
for matter
for movement
or
for action.

November 1947.

I do not accept
I am never going to forgive anyone
that I've been <u>whored alive</u>
throughout all of my existence

and that
happened solely because of the fact
that it's <u>me</u>
who was god
really, verifiably, god

me, a man
and not that so-called spirit
who was never more than the projection into the
    clouds
of the body of a man other than me
and he
proclaimed himself the
    Creator of the World

And the hideous story of that Creator of the World
you know it

It's the story of that body
who <u>pursued</u> (he didn't follow behind) my own
    body
and who, in order to appear foremost and to be born
projected himself through my own body

and
    was able to be born
through the eventration of my own body

from which he kept a fragment upon him
in order
    to be able to pass himself off
as me

Him
    a malevolent body
which all spatial dimensions wanted nothing of

me
    a body in the act of creating itself
and consequently not yet having reached the state
    of completion
but which was evolving
towards integral purity
and not towards integral impiety
as with that impiety of the so-called Creator of the
    World
who knew himself to be inadmissible
but wanting anyway, at any cost, to be able to live
could find nothing better
    in order to <u>take on being</u>
than to live at the cost of
    my assassination

In spite of everything, my body remade itself
against,
and by passing through, a thousand assaults of evil
    and of hatred
which, each time, deteriorated my body
and left me for dead

and in that way, through the strength of having
    died
I ended up by achieving a real immortality
And
    this is the true history of events
    in the way that they really took place
    and
    not
as they are perceived through some kind of legend-
    ary atmosphere of myths
which serve to set reality askew
but

this true history, which is my own, is a dreadful
    one
it's the story
    of a man
who wanted
    to be pure
    and good
but
    whom
      nobody ever wanted
because human beings have never been able to
    make deals with anything other than
    impurity
    impiety
    injustice
    and acts of assassination
It's already so difficult to be
    pure
but when you have to be pure in confrontation with
    the generalised ill will
amassed entirely in league against you
– and which does everything it can, by means of
    force, to confine you within evil –
all that becomes a desperately difficult task

And I'm alone.
Have I ever been able to find ten people who wanted
    to follow me?
I don't even know the answer to that
but in any case
    not a single one
up until now
    has ever manifested themself to me.

And furthermore –
I've lost my health, since the age of 19 years old
I'm now 52 years old
and
    unless some kind of miracle takes place

there's no chance now that I'll ever be able to
    recover it.
52 years old –
for a man living in ordinary conditions
that's the start of his decline
he's reaching the entryway to the grave
Anyone who hasn't <u>lived prior to</u> that age is not
    going to be able to think that he has any life left

but I'm not living in ordinary conditions
I did not enter into this world through the gates of
    the habitual matrix
my birth: that was a horrendous struggle
        an act of abysmal warfare
        an extreme sin

I was swimming in a river of pus
which never existed
but which was conjured-up right there, and thrown
    at me
to prevent me from passing through
and the body
    the obscene body
of that humanity wanted to close down its stitching
    around me
when my own body had already been made
and had no need of anything, nor of anybody
except just a little span of time
    to exist

Moreover, before I had this body
I was something that existed in nature
a kind of essential, driving-force organ
that had no need of the state of being
and was going to shake it off

because a man is not a being

a true man has no sexual organ
he knows nothing of that terrifying horror
and of that stupefying sin
what he does know is the state of final achievement
which being
– by its definition –
will never know about

Moreover: that man is going to be what I want
a pure body
and not
a pure spirit

a pure body
– and the hole of that virgin of catholic priests
will be deployed as the receptacle for the dropped-
     down shit from those pure spirits

That's because it has to be a spirit that
     shits
a <u>pure</u> body cannot
     shit

What that body does shit out
is the coagulation of spirits
which is in a frenzy to steal something from that
     body
because, without a body, it's impossible to exist
The body, that's going to be what I made it
with my habitual breath, every day
yes, I am
     the only one
          who merited it.

Solely that merit gives you the right of entry into a
     body
the merit of having won that body
elbow against elbow
and finger by finger

and not
    by having lived
as has the 'Creator of the World'
with
    a body that was stolen
        through a criminal act of infiltration
– a body which
    was precisely
    engaged in the process
    of meriting <u>itself</u>

    by rolling itself around
    little by little
    in the horrendous cooked-up piss-up

But, once that cooking-up was all done
all that remained for my body was to harden up
to plug up my accomplished effort
but that's what I haven't had the time to be able to
    do

A life like the one
that I've lived since the age of 19 years old
has given to me
that capacity to plug up
but
    the need
which the being revealed, and signified, to me, in
    1915
means that now I can't live even one more day
without opium

But, we're now in the year 1947 –

so then, that makes up a total of 32 years
    of expectation
        <u>and of struggles</u>

December 1947.

*

There does not exist the fullness
there only exists the void
there does not exist the void
there only exists the fullness
me: my entire resistance
– I'm egg-less –
is beyond the void and the fullness

   o bambul
   atchi bambul
   ro bambul
   atchum

I am the source
but I can also
I can stop
rectify
create detours for
replenish
that source

a certain thing
without an above nor a below
without an outside nor an inside
and which is not a circle
and which is not a plan
and which is not the blackskinned chicken
made dirty and black by the strikings of every plan

September 1947.

*

And if I'm now talking about the putting into ques-
    tion of the last judgement
it's because I realised
– not so long ago –
that there never even has been any first judgement

nobody has been judged by anybody, before their
    birth
with the consequence that the entire world and
    everyone in it
is born
in a state of sheer arbitrariness
and from that state of arbitrariness
Nobody has asked anybody:
Why are you being born?
And where are you coming from?
And where are you going to?

And that's why
everything is going so badly, in a world that is itself
    terribly unmade

We're living,
in the subterraneas of our unconscious,
with I don't know what kinds of interjections
– interjected by the world of science
    or
    by the church –
of I don't know what kind of judgement, cast upon
    the soul being born
and which arose in the first fishy stenches
of I don't know what mythology of Argos or of
    Mongolia-Tibet
and it's as though the act of being born has already
    stank, for a long time, of death

what this implies
is our breathed-in ignorance

our seething, malevolent ignorance about this very
matter.
But I believe that we are, all of us, dead fish,
fish maddened to be born from the sea of the
     immense infinity
– surrealist psychology! –
I believe we are the dead who exist beneath the dead
and we stink of a horrendous shit
even before we are made to pass through the ocular
     eye of the police
that eye, so infinite, and which weighs so heavily
     upon us

and for which, we're nothing but miserable shit,
     and invisible
not worth bothering about for two pennies
shit-misfired non-entities
dirty little infections of the void testicles
and
filth-infused testicular half-wits

I think you must be bothering that eye
by having fucked up a pair of balls, for it
and some shit, that now has to be swallowed
through the entrails of its nose
and
I believe that's the real truth
the raw, true and evident
true truth of the truth,

Because I have an index finger that's been deeply
     implanted
– it said –
in order to stir up pain in his entrails
but that's not the real purpose, since I've also stuck
     into there a walled-up thumb

and on that thumb

the hammered-in nail of the pointing index finger
    of the nail to hammer in – which is just what I am

since before all eternity

and which a hundred billion nails of miserable shit-
    denizens are being hammered into

by myriads of billions of numbers of the baseless
    Myrmidons
against the walls of the infinite chestnut-fist
which only finally came to know
that it was a body
and that body
is nothing other

than the body of my own body

raw, infinite, against the sign and out of line,

and it came to know that even the boundary-less
    infinity
has a boundary

in the end

because even infinity is dead
'infinity' is the name of a dead man
who isn't dead
but for whose reawakening you are going to have to
    wait
until there are enough of the dead
and that will happen only through the replication
    of this nail of death, hammered-in
and which is hammered-into my hand's black palm
upon the mountain of the dead cats

they're dead, those cats, because the cunt who's
    sleeping

weds the caterwauling of the female black cat
who bit her husband
when he manufactured for her a child
a child that is going to bite both the small and the
     great
snotting-out illness into the rolling of the dead
     daughters' entrails
which are long, long as a true infinity

what that means is that I'm telling the story of that
     infamous christian
who made himself into a jew, to wed his son

so, that lascivious rascal, he's called the dirty beggar
which means
daughter of the octopus
opening of the gaping mouth

CAI MATARNA
ORA MATTA
ONGUE METTER
TODER SOCQUÉ
SOQUE
SOCQUETTE
AND SOCQETTÉ
your double stops you dead
– and the head-crucified
who bites only at his own toes
was nothing other than christ, with his gang of
     scum
because 'christ', in Hebrew, if you chase after it,
means 'a donkey's fart'
and Jesus Christ
was truly the issue of that donkey's fart
that evil-smelling toxic gas of the ass's anus
and he was only ever crucified in spirit
while his body
peeled itself away
and, through greed,

and stickiness,
burst itself outwards
by the joy of precious stones
of that <u>lotus</u>
which the anus forms
when it rises up from the table
because the anus, sat down, is there at the table
and it's there that it's eating up its plaits

and in the name of jesus christ
thank you

30 September 1947.

*

5 or 6 people need to come and turn around me,
like animals
that search and scratch around in the ground

because the words that I'm speaking form exactly
    that ground which I'm now digging into
in order that the true ones can search out, here
what they will be able to discover, here, that is of the
    best, in the infinity of the world to be created
these bodies that have been so badly cut-together,
squared-off so badly, in this past time
in which they were nothing but a kind of <u>bloating-
    up</u>

and not a body that has been sculpted down into an
    object
as will happen now
here, inside here
in this theatre that I'm creating for you.

*

THE THEATRE OF CRUELTY

Do you know anything more outrageously shit-laden
than the story of God
and of his being: SATAN,
the heart's membrane,
the ignominious sow,
of the illusory universal
and who, from his dribbling teats
has only ever hidden
the Void
from us?

Confronted with this idea of a universe that is pre-
established
human beings have never, up to now, succeeded
in establishing their superiorety over the vast
domains of possibility.

Because, if there's nothing,
there really is nothing
but this excremental idea
of a being who, for example, is supposed to have
created the beasts.

And in that case,
where do the beasts come from?
From that the world of corporeal perceptions
hasn't achieved what it plans,
and is still incomplete,

from that there's a mental life
but no true organic life,
from that the simple idea of a pure organic life
can even present itself,

from that it's been possible
for a distinction to be drawn between
pure organic nascent life
and the life that is heated-up
and integrally concrete, of the human body.

The human body is an electric battery
whose charges have been drained away and
　　　suppressed,

whose capacities and distinctions
have been directed towards sexual life
when that body is created
precisely to absorb
through its voltaic movements
all of the erratic opennesses
of the void's infinity,
of the void's apertures
– that are becoming more and more expansive –
of an organic possibility that has never been
　　　fulfilled.

The human body has its need to eat,
but who has ever tried to direct the expansive
　　　capacities of appetites other than towards the
　　　domain of sexual life?

You have to make the human anatomy dance,
　　　finally,

from on high to down low and from down low to
　　　on high,
from backward to frontward and
from frontward to backward,
but it has to be much more from the back, to the
　　　back,
moreover, than from the backward to the
　　　frontward,

that way the problem of the depletion
of nutritional commodities,
will no longer need to be resolved,
because it is not going to have to
even present itself.

The human body was forced to eat,
forced to drink,
only in order to avoid
making it dance.
It was forced to fuck the occult
only in order to make it exempt itself
from pressurising
and from tormenting occult life.

Because there's nothing
so much as that so-called occult life
that is in need of being tormented.

It's there that God, and his being,
thought that they could flee from the demented
    man,
there, in the domain of occult life that is more and
    more absent
that's where God wanted to make human beings
    believe
that everything can be perceived, and seized,
    through the mind,
when all that there is, that is existent and real,
is the physical exterior life
and everything that flees from that life or diverts
    itself away from it
cannot be other than the limbo of the world of
    demons.

And God wanted to make human beings believe in
    the reality of that world of demons.

But, the world of demons is absent.
It is not going to coincide with what can be proven.
The best means to cure yourself of it
and to destroy it
is to accomplish reality's construction.
Because reality is not accomplished,
it's still not been constructed.
The return of an eternal health
in the world of eternal life
depends upon that act of accomplishment.

The theatre of cruelty
is not the symbol of an absent void,
of some kind of horrendous incapacity of human
    beings to accomplish their lives for themselves,
It's instead the affirmation
of a terrible
necessity that is, moreover, inescapable.

Upon the never-visited mountain slopes
of the Caucasus,
of the Carpathians,
of the Himalayas,
of the Apennines,
there take place every day,
night and day,
– and already for years and years –
horrendous corporeal rituals
where the blackened life
life that is forever beyond any control, and
    blackened
devotes itself to horrendous, repulsive feasting.
There, limbs and organs
– those reputed to be in some way abject
because they're perpetually being expelled,
and forced away
beyond the capacities of external lyrical life –
are put to use in all the delirium of an uncon-
    strained eroticism,

and in the middle of an outpouring
– more and more compelling
and virginal –
of a liquor
whose nature it's never been possible to classify,
because, more and more, it is beyond the created,
     beyond the self.

(I'm not speaking especially about the sexual organ,
     or the anus
– which, moreover, are going to have to be hacked
     off and liquidated –
but also the tops of the thighs,
of the haunches,
of the loin-meat,
of the stomach, total and sex-less
and of the navel)

At this instant, all of that is sexual and obscene
because that's never been able to be worked-at,
     nurtured, to render it beyond the obscene
and the bodies that are dancing there
cannot be separated from the obscene,
they've systematically wedded themselves to
     obscene life
but it's now imperative to destroy
that dance of the obscene bodies
in order to replace them with the dance
of our own bodies.

For years now
I've been driven frantic
and been malevolently frozen
by the dance of a horrendous world of microbes
– exclusively sexualised microbes –
among which I've been able to recognise,
in those particular spaces' life of forced coercion,
men, women
and children of modern existence.

I have been endlessly tormented by being eaten-up
    with intolerable eczemas
through which all of the abscess-bloated states of
    the erotic life of the coffin
accorded themselves a total freedom of action.

You don't need to look any further than those black
    ritual dances
for the origin of all eczemas,
of all rashes,
of all bouts of tuberculosis,
of all epidemics,
of all plagues
in the face of which modern medicine
– more and more driven into bewilderment –
shows itself to be powerless, in finding the required
    cauterisation.

For ten years now,
my sensibility has been forced down
the steps of the most monstrous sarcophagi,
those of the still-incapacitated world of the dead
and also of the living who wanted –
(and at the point we're at, it can be only by vice)
who wanted to live as the dead.

But, very simply, I am going to avoid getting ill
and with me,
there'll be that world which is all that I know.

    O PEDANA
    NA KOMEV TAU DEDANA
    TAU KOMEV

    NA DEDANU
    NA KOMEV
    TAU KOMEV
    NA COME
    COPSI TRA

KA FIGA ARONDA

KA LAKEOU
TO COBBRA

COBRA JA
JA FUTSA MATA

OF the serpent that's not here
A NA

Because you've let the organisms stick out their tongue
it became necessary that the organisms' tongue
be cut off
at the exit of the body's tunnels.

Plague,
cholera,
hemorrhagic smallpox
exist
solely because dance
– and by consequence, theatre –
have not yet begun to exist.

Is there any doctor,
of the deprived bodies of our contemporary misery,
who has really tried to observe cholera up close?

It's to be done by listening to the breathing or the
    pulse of a sick person,
by applying the ear towards those embodied
    concentration camps, those deprived bodies of
    misery,
towards the beatings of feet, of torsos, of sexual
    organs
of the immense, suppressed terrain
of certain terrible microbes
which are
other human bodies.

Whereabouts are they?
At this level, or else in the subterraneas
of certain tombs
in locations that are historically
if not also geographically unsuspected.

    KO EMBACH
    TU UR JA BELLA
    UR JA BELLA

    KOU EMBACH

It's there that the living arrange to meet up
with the dead
and numerous paintings of the 'dance of death'
have their sole origin in that.
Those are uprisings
in which two outlandish worlds' conjoinings cease-
    lessly depict themselves
and the painting of the Middle Ages
along with all painting, moreover,
all history
and I could even say
all geography
were created out of that.

The earth is painting itself and it's depicting itself
driven by the action of a terrible dance
to which has not yet been accorded
epidemically
all of its manifestations.

POST-SCRIPTUM

Wherever there is metaphysics,
mysticism,
irreducible dialectics,
I listen out
for the convulsion

of the large intestine
of my hunger
and under the propulsions of that hunger's sombre
    life
I dictate to my hands
    their dance,
    to my feet
    or to my arms.

The theatre and the sung-out dance,
are the theatre of furious revolts
emerging from the human body's misery
to confront the problems which it cannot enter into
or of which the passive,
    or spurious
    or ergot-ridden
    or impenetrable
    or obscured
    character
    exceeds that body.

It's then that it dances
in soul-blocks of
KHA, KHA

that are infinitely more arid,
but organic too;
the body rectifies
the black wall
from its slippages away from the inside of the heart;

the world of larvae without backbones
from which the endless night detaches itself,
the world of useless insects:
    lice,
    fleas,
    bedbugs,
    mosquitoes,
    spiders,

only proliferates
because the everyday body
has lost, through hunger,
its originating cohesion
and it loses, through gusts
    through mountains
    through gangs
    through endless theories
the black and bitter smoulderings
of the rages
of its energy.

POST-SCRIPTUM

Who am I?
Where do I come from?
I am Antonin Artaud
and as I say this
I know how to say this
immediately
you will see my current body
burst into fragments
and reconstruct itself
under ten thousand infamous aspects
a new body
through which you will
never be able
to forget me.

*

It's me
    the Man
who will be the judge
at the end of the day
it's towards me
that all of the elements
of the body and of all things

are going to come to adapt themselves
it's <u>the state</u> of my
body which will make
the Last Judgement

*

Where am I going, towards the infinite?
what is it, what is the void?

where have I come from, from the infinite
what was it, that void burdened down by something

By what?

by god
and what is that?

an idea of worlds with worlds

what needs to be done is to reduce down all of that
and rediscover the pure infinite

*

In the guise of
the choice of a
body
I say shit
to everything
and
   I
     sleep.

*

It's getting very
cold now
as when

it's
Artaud
the dead man
who
breathes

*

Yes, even at this time
we've reached, there are still doctors
who will think
that you are mad
because you are mad
and that madness
is...

*

This morning
I – who invented everything
I understood for the first time
the difference
between a sensation
and a feeling:
in the sensation
you take what comes
in the feeling
you intervene.

*

I am going to need to rediscover a particular way I
used to have of invoking the subterranean forces
of my SELF, as the best and the most exceptional
forces of myself that I was inviting to resurge
o makala o moskendin zeta.

*

Y-a temimazza
Khantun stara

ya temara
hantum schasura

I've condemned the child
from the middle of the sea
with my finger
placed against my stomach at that point where
    Satan passed through
in order to repel away Satan

then I took myself away back to the middle of the
    heavens.

               *

Do what is evil
do all evil
    and
commit many sins
but do not do evil to me
do not touch me
    me
do not make me do evil
    to myself
or I will revenge myself for it, cruelly
you can befoul and debase
    god
he has got nothing left to lose
he has already committed every dirty act
    so, no evil done to me
    no evil around me
    no evil where I am <u>me</u>
so that I can live
    in a world
        that is pure

so that I can have around
    me
            the pure ones
        the pure heroes.

                            *

It's not possible, at the end, that the miracle won't
    burst out
I have been tortured, too much
I have been troubled at the world, too much
I have worked hard to be pure and strong, too much
I have hunted down evil, too much
I have searched to have a body of my own, too
    much

                            *

The question
    that
    counts
    is that of
    of
    the I
    in movement
    to you
while passing through the arcades
over their main beams'
intercrossings.

                            *

I am making a weapon of my right arm
I am making a weapon of my right arm

And the blow
did not leave
the blow which, on that evening
destroyed it all

and the blow has not
left
and the body has not left

he
will leave
suddenly
tonight
at an
unforeseen
instant

50 dessins
pour

apprivoiser
la
magie

si un bruit à l'école

50 DRAWINGS TO ASSASSINATE MAGIC

31 JANUARY 1948

50 Drawings to assassinate magic – the first of Artaud's two major texts of the last weeks of his life – concerns the pencil drawings which he incorporated into his notebooks, image against text, text against image. It is the residue of an unrealized book project proposed to Artaud by the gallery owner Pierre Loeb; Artaud chose the notebooks from which he intended to take the fifty drawings to be incorporated into the book, but not the particular drawings themselves. Loeb took the project no further after Artaud's death, though the text was eventually published by Gallimard in 2004. *50 Drawings to assassinate magic* is the last of Artaud's three extended texts about his own artworks (following *Ten years that language has been gone*, from April 1947, and *The Human Face*, from June 1947, written for the brochure accompanying Artaud's exhibition of his drawings at Loeb's gallery in July 1947).

This translation was made directly from the original manuscript notebook, catalogued as number 396 of 406, at the Bibliothèque nationale de France, with the support of the curator Guillaume Fau. The notebook is pierced through from cover to cover, with incisions from a knife, wielded with great force, eleven times, leaving holes which serve to indicate that the notebook was assaulted even before Artaud started writing in it, since he takes care to avoid writing in those incisions. The text has erratic punctuation, retained here, and appears to stop dead in its tracks at several points; this version would not have been the text's final version if the planned book had gone ahead, and Artaud would certainly have reworked it and dictated the final version vocally, as he preferred to do. Notebook 396 also holds a number of fragments and glossolalia inscribed both before and after *50 Drawings to assassinate magic*; they are also included here, since they work to illuminate or to inflect the main text.

50 Drawings

to assassinate magic

Here, it's not a matter of
drawings
in the strict sense of the word
of some kind of incorporation
of reality through the drawing.
They are not an experiment
aiming at renewing
the art
– which I never believed in anyway –
of drawing
no
but in order to understand them
first you have to be clear about them
These are 50 drawings
taken from notebooks of
literary,
poetic
psychological,
physiological
magical
notes
magical especially
magical first of all
and above all
They are, then, interwoven
with the pages,
embedded upon the pages
where the writing
holds pre-eminence for
vision,

writing
feverish noting,
effervescent,
burning
    blasphemy
    cursing.
From curse towards
curse
these pages
advance
and as bodies with
a new
sensibility
these drawings
are there
to comment on them
    to give them air
    and to illuminate them
These are not drawings
they figure nothing,
disfigure nothing,
are not there in order to
construct
build up
institute
a world
even an abstract one
They are notes,
words,
supporting pillars,
because they're burning,
    corrosive
    incisive
    spurted out
    from some kind of
    whirlwind
    of vitriol
under the jaw
under the blade

they are there as though
nailed down
and destined not to
move any further
so, supporting pillars
but which are going to generate
their own apocalypse
because they've said too much
to be born
and too much in being born
not to be reborn
and to take on their body
authentically   then

But all of that,
would be nothing
if you had to
just leave it there,
and not get out of
the written
page
subsequently illustrated
by the light
of these drawings
that is somehow flickering
which intends to say nothing
and represents
absolutely nothing

In order to understand these drawings
in their entirety
    you have to
    1. get out of the written page
        to enter into
        the real
        but
    2. get out of the real
        to enter into
        the surreal,

the extra-real
the beyond-the-real
the beyond-the-perceptible
that's what these drawings
never cease
to plunge into
because that's where they emerged from,
and to understand that, in fact, they are nothing
but the commentary
of an action which
has really
taken place,
and which the figuration
upon paper
delineates
with a surge
which has taken place
and has generated
its effects
magnetically and
magically,
and because these are
not drawings, the
representation
or the
figuration
of an object
of a state of
the head or the eye
of an element
and of a psychological
event,
they are purely
and simply the
reproduction upon the
paper,
of a magical
gesture
which I've exerted

into the true space
with the breath of my
lungs
and my hands,
with my head
and my 2 feet
with my torso and my
arteries etc, –

When I write,
in general
I write my notes
just at one stroke
but that's
not enough for me,
and I seek to prolong
the action of what
I've written in
the atmosphere, so then
I get to work
I search out
    consistencies,
    matches
    with the sounds,
with the oscillations of the body
and of the limbs
which will create an action,
which will call upon
the surrounding spaces
to rise up
and to speak
then I get close
to the written
page
and
     ...
but I've been forgetting to
say that those
consistencies

have their meaning,
[note: a line is erased here]
I breathe out, I sing out,
I make variations
but not just by chance
    no
I always possess
a kind of prodigious subject
or a world
to create and call up

yes, I know
the creative
objective value of the breath,
the breath that is some-
thing in the air
    it's not
    only
air that has been
stirred up
it's an immense concretising
in the
air
and which has
to be felt
within the body and
through the body
as with a great amassing
that is, in itself, atomic
of elements
and of limbs
which right at that moment
makes up the drawing.
A substance
very far beyond
that of barley-
sugar
and born right in that moment
there

instantaneously
within the body,

electri-
cal matter
which would be able
to explain
– if it was
itself
explicable –
the nature
of certain atomic
gases
of certain
atoms in a state of repulsion
I'm talking about atoms now
just as I can say
a section of a wall,
a volcano's interior surface,
the molten artery of a
volcano,
a great wall of lava in
movement towards an
upending of
what will become the immediate,

so, my drawings reproduce
    these forms
    that are made apparent by them,
    these worlds of
    prodigies,
    these objects
    by which the Way
    is established
    and what used to be
called the great alchemical work
is from now onwards
pulverised, because we
are no longer involved in

chemistry
but instead in
nature
and I really believe
that
nature itself
is going to speak out

<u>Antonin Artaud</u>
31 January 1948

Texts preceding
50 Drawings
to assassinate magic
in Artaud's notebook 396

Yes   magic exists.
In fact
it's all that exists
in this world
<u>that is fabricated by it</u>
and then
lost by it
but for nothing
in the world   it doesn't
want that
that
that *that*
is known.

That's why
it gets people
locked up

like me
those who have sniffed out
that thing

who have become
aware
and who talk about it
in insane asylums

There exists I don't know
what kind of
ceremonial magic
with bangs and crashes

by which you can
rise up

to the level of being able to see
celestial life
but I'm not going to talk about that here

that
offers
no interest
to me.

There's another magic
with or without ceremony
but which acts

this magic,
the ugliest, most sordid and
vile magic that can be conceived of
is entirely based
on the action
of one man against another man
of one group   against another
group
and that's the only magic
that
I want to
be concerned with
here.
Because the
world
is dying from it
that's really it
and because we are dying from it

all of us little by little
meanly and nastily

30 January 1948
Everything, that emerges
from my paralytic fingers
acts
with a marvelous
and rightful effectiveness

My contempt for doctors,
for educators,
for artists

is necessary,
but it's been lacking
ever since I've
exerted less
rapidity
acrimony
into it
having already been assassinated 2 times
<u>with that aim</u>...

It's getting very
cold now
as when
it's
Artaud
the dead man
who
breathes

31 January 1948
That everything   Half past one
in the morning
Afghanistan
Kabul above all
needs to be

driven away
with the exception
of the
one and only
Neneka
depicted already 1,000 times

this action is
bewitching
furious
implacable
atrocious.
It's not trying to deal with anything
neither is it preoccupied
with anything

50 drawings
to
assassinate
magic
the <u>text</u>
follows here

TEXTS FOLLOWING
50 DRAWINGS
TO ASSASSINATE MAGIC
IN ARTAUD'S NOTEBOOK 396

the   meeting
of the   tower of
Babel   with the
tower   of Pisa
50   thousand
centuries   later

ibi
kayar
kaman

ta ema
aman
ta ema
ema
natar

THE NEW *TUTUGURI*

16 FEBRUARY 1948

Artaud's final major text – the new *Tutuguri* – emerged as an unforeseen replacement for a previous text, *Tutuguri: the rite of the black sun*, from October 1947, which was included to be recorded for Artaud's planned radio programme *To have done with the judgement of god*, and was performed on 29 November 1947 by Maria Casarès. After the programme's censorship on 1 February 1948, an immediate plan was launched by the publisher K to publish all of its texts as a small book. *Tutuguri: the rite of the black sun* had already been promised by Artaud to Marc Barbezat, so to replace it he then had to write a new *Tutuguri* text, and did so, with evident speed and the erratic use of punctuation retained here, within the span of a letter written to Barbezat on 16 February 1948. In that letter, Artaud especially emphasises the text's direct emergence from his previous day's haemorrhages.

The publisher – and pharmaceutical factory owner – Marc Barbezat (1913–99) was based outside Paris, in Décines near Lyon; he first published Artaud's work in 1947 in his large-format magazine 'L'Arbalète', and in 1955 collected Artaud's writings on his 1936 journey to Mexico and his experiences there with the Tarahumara people, as *Les Tarahumaras*. Barbezat is now best-known as an early publisher of Jean Genet's work. The new *Tutuguri* appeared in 1955 in *Les Tarahumaras* and in 1989 in a book assembled by Barbezat, *l'arve et l'aume suivi de 24 lettres à Marc Barbezat*, where it is positioned within the context of Artaud's letter, whose opening and closing pages focus mainly on ongoing publishing quar-rels. Barbezat's archive of his work with Artaud is held at the Institut Mémoires de l'édition contempo-raine (IMEC) research centre, at the Ardenne abbey in Saint-Germain-la-Blanche-Herbe, near Caen in northern France; this text was translated from the original manuscript letter with the support of IMEC's research director, Albert Dichy.

THE NEW *TUTUGURI*

<u>Tutuguri</u> is a black ritual, performed for the external glory of the sun.

It's the Ritual of the black night and of the <u>eternal</u> death of the sun.

No, the sun is not going to be coming back

and in reality the six crosses forming the circle to be traversed by the celestial body are there solely to bar the sun's way, because we don't know enough – we know nothing about this, here in Europe – about how the cross is a black sign, we don't know enough about the '<u>salivating power of the cross</u>', and about how the cross forms an ejecting of saliva exerted over words of thought.

In Mexico the cross and the sun belong together, and the leaping sun is this turning sentence which takes place six times before it reveals itself,

so the cross is a heinous sign and it has to be that its matter burns – why heinous – it's because the tongue engaged in salivating the sign is a heinous one,

and why is it salivating the sign?

In order to anoint it.

No saintly or sacred sign can exist if it hasn't been anointed.

But isn't the tongue – at the moment of that anointing – itself stuck out into a point?

Isn't it positioning itself between the 4 cardinal points?

So as the sun appears, it needs to jump over the six points of the heinous sentence to be saved, for which it generates a kind of translation in the form of lightning.

Because the sun really appears right at the base of the crosses as though as a ball of lightning,

and that lightning is never going to grant forgiveness?

What is it never going to forgive?

The sins of the people and of the surrounding village – and it's for that reason that, for several weeks before the ritual, you can see the Tarahumara people engaged in purifying themselves, and dressing in clean, white clothes.

And now the day of the Ritual, with its lightning-striking apparitions, is finally here.

It's then that six men dressed in their white clothes – the six men considered to be the purest of the tribe – are positioned right at ground-level.

And each of them is supposed to have become wedded to a cross.

One of those crosses is made of two sticks tied together with a filthy cord. And there's a seventh man standing there, holding a cross against himself, attached to his thigh, with between his hands an instrument to make outlandish music, made of an accumulation of wooden slats, one on top of the other,

and which gives out a sound somewhere between a bell and a cannon.

And so on a certain day, at sunrise, the seventh Tutuguri initiates the dance by beating on one of the slats with a deep-black, cast-iron hammer,

then you see the men with their crosses shoot up as though directly out of the earth, advancing while hopping, to form a circle, and each of them has to manifest his cross seven times without at any point breaking that intact circle.

I don't know if it's because the wind is rising now,

or if a wind has arisen from that music from another time which is still persisting today,

but you feel as though whipped by a gust from

the night, by a breath of air that's risen up out of the vaults of an abolished humanity and which came to show its face here,

a face which is painted, a figure that is grinning and merciless.

Merciless – because the justice it's bringing isn't of this world here:

Be pure and chaste

it seems to be saying.

Be virginal too.

or else I'll be unleashing my gehenna upon you.

And gehenna is starting to unleash itself too.

The 7th Tutuguri's cacophony has taken on an atrocious propulsion: it's the crater of a volcano bursting into its eruption.

The wooden slats seem to be breaking under the noise as though they were a forest devastated by blows wielded by some ferocious woodcutter.

And then, what you had been expecting suddenly happens: fumes that are sulphurous and <u>lilac-coloured</u> emerge as a mass from a point in the circle traced by the six men,

and which the six crosses

have sealed shut,

and from under those fumes, a flame, an immense

flame,

is illuminated

– suddenly –

and that immense flame is now <u>seething</u>.

It's seething with a noise that is <u>unheard-of</u>.
Its interior fills up with stars and incandescent corpuscles – it's as though the arrival of the sun has brought with it a celestial system.

And now you can see that the sun has taken its rightful position.

It has manifested itself in the middle of the celestial system. It's positioned itself immediately as though at the very centre, in an amazing outbursting.

Because the flaming corpuscles, as with the sol-
diers of an army engaged in warfare, have thrown
themselves one onto the other, while bursting.

And now the sun has become round. And you
can see an igneous ball in the axis itself of the natu-
ral sun – since it's sunrise – a ball that rises up and
jumps from cross to cross.

The six men have now opened their arms, not
in order to signify the cross, but with their hands
outstretched, as though they wanted to receive that
ball, and that ball is turning around each of the
crosses implanted in the earth, in a perpetual act of
refusal.

Because the cacophony is a wind, it's now
become as though it were the base of a wind
through which an army could very well advance
forward.

And in effect,

There is, at the borders of noise and of the void,
because the noise is now so strong that the void is
all that it calls up in advance of itself.

There is, then, an intense stamping. The rhythm
of an army on the march, punctuated by the gallop
of a panic-stricken charge.

The ball of fire has burned up the six crosses,
the six men – with their arms outstretched and
who have seen that thing arrive – are now, all six of
them

exhausted and drooling.

And the noise of galloping is at a maddening point.

And you can see on the horizon above the
crosses a kind of enraged horse which is advancing

with a naked man upon it

because the rhythm's beating was 7.

But there are only six crosses.

And in the wood-driven cacophony of the 7th
Tutuguri

there's still an introduction of nothingness,

there's still this introduction of nothingness,

this time hollowed-out,
a time that is hollowed-out,
a kind of exhausting voiding between the blades
of wood that cut;
nothingness, that calls up the torso of the man,
the body of the man cut into segments
in the fury (no: in the fervour)
of the things of the interior.
There, where underneath the void
the noise of great bells in the wind,
the tearing-apart of marine guns,
the wailing of waves in the hot Southern
windstorms
choose their places;
now to cut it short, the horse in advancing car-
ries upon itself the torso of a man, of a naked man
who is brandishing
not a cross, but a stave of wood and iron,
attached to a gigantic horseshoe
through which his entire body passes,
his body marked with a gash of blood,
and the horseshoe is right there, like the clamp-
ing jaws
of a straitjacket,
in which the man is caught
at the gash of his blood.
Ivry-sur-Seine, 16 February 1948
<u>Tutuguri</u>

<u>Antonin Artaud</u>

ARTAUD'S
LAST LETTERS

JANUARY–FEBRUARY 1948

Translated here are seven of Artaud's handwritten letters from the final weeks of his life; other letters exist from those weeks, while others are lost or have disappeared from sight. These seven letters – among the last of many thousands written over Artaud's lifetime – are addressed to the writer and editor Jean Paulhan, to the radio producers Fernand Pouey and René Guignard (Pouey commissioned Artaud's radio programme *To have done with the judgement of god*, while Guignard was its sound engineer), to his friend Paule Thévenin who participated as a performer in that recording, and to the publisher Marc Barbezat. Artaud's letters of his last months were always written very rapidly, often in métro trains or buses or while standing in the street, as well as at his pavilion in Ivry-sur-Seine. That great speed reinforced their frequent lack of punctuation and capital letters, retained in these translations.

In the letters, Artaud is especially preoccupied with the censoring of his radio broadcast and with the two private events (the second, on 23 February 1948, held at a Paris cinema, the 'Washington') at which friends of Artaud – and writers, artists and journalists – were able to hear the recording; prior to the second of those events, Artaud demanded that cuts be made to the recording to accentuate its sonic elements, though the producers neglected to carry through his demands. Artaud also invokes his recent and ongoing texts, some of which were sold simultaneously to several publishers, causing discord. Artaud is preoccupied too with expanding his supply of drugs, and appears awestruck when the doctor he consulted about his abdominal pain, at Paris's Salpêtrière hospital, Professor Henri Mondor, authorises him to have as much opium as he wants. In these letters, Artaud is planning to leave the Ivry-sur-Seine clinic for Antibes, but died eleven days before his date of departure.

Ivry, 16 January 1948

My very dear Jean Paulhan,

You now have to make a decision <u>urgently</u>, everything is pressing now.

4 days ago I had another attack in front of my fireplace. I fell down, sustained a horrendous wound to the knee and caught my arm underneath my body, all of which has led to paralysis on my right side.

The doctor at the Ivry convalescence home told me these attacks were due to the <u>lack</u> of opium but his pharmacist refused to give him any for me.

But I have the chance to locate some in Marseille – I can't go there myself but Mrs Thévenin would be able to go.

But that requires an advance payment of 80 thousand francs, including the travel costs.

I'm asking you to prepare a letter to Mr Dauchez so that he will advance that sum to Mrs Thévenin in order that she can make that journey and buy the merchandise. She would be able to leave next week.

Your dear friend,

Antonin Artaud

Ivry sur Seine, 7 February 1948

Mr Jean Paulhan
Dear friend,

I've rented a villa
in Antibes,
from the date of 15 March
for three months.
That cost me 18,000 francs which I've paid in advance
using the sums of my royalty payments for
<u>Van Gogh</u>
Artaud the mômo,
<u>Here lies</u>
and that accursed Radio-Broadcast:
<u>To have done with the judgement of god</u>.
However, since my stay at the Convalescence home
will lapse from that date of 15 March, the sum to be
accorded to me by Mr Dauchez will now be needed
to pay for my meals in Antibes and for the cleaning
woman I'm going to hire there.
You know already that Mrs Paule Thévenin is going
to accompany me for the start of my settling-in there
and will watch over me.
She is planning to stay with me for 1 and a half
months. After that, her sister, or else Marthe Robert,
will replace her.
In that way I won't be alone and I will be able to have
the total rest which all of the doctors have recom-
mended for me.
Yesterday at the Salpêtrière I met with Doctor Profes-
sor Mondor.

He found that I was in a horrendous state and banned me from doing all work. He told me that I now had to live *lying down* and that the very most I could do was dictate my texts, in view of my horrendous fatigue.

But what is most remarkable is that he agreed to write letters to my doctors telling them that, given my current state, there was no need to bother about any detoxification and that opium has now become an essential and necessary thing for me. And that I will have to take it <u>every day</u>.

As you know, this is what we have all been looking for: to have such a certificate coming from an official medical expert. So at last – this result has been obtained. And I believe that I will finally be able to go to Antibes and have some peaceful rest.

Very warmly,

<u>Antonin Artaud</u>

Ivry sur Seine, 10 February 1948

My very dear friend,

1 copy,
of <u>Artaud the Mômo</u>
signed and dedicated by my own hand,
and
1 copy
of
HERE LIES preceded by
THE INDIAN CULTURE
were sent to you at least 15 days if not 3 weeks ago,
if you haven't received them, it's because the office
receptionist at the N.R.F. has got hold of them and
you now have to do everything to demand them
back at all costs
because I did what was needed from my side
and
signed those copies with my own hand
<u>specifically for you</u>.
They must have been cast aside in some office or
other.
These copies which I arranged to be sent to you are
on SPECIAL PAPER
but – I'm telling you this again – all of that happened
nearly three weeks ago
so there must be someone who has got their hands
on them before they reached you, and you have to
get searching now and demand them back
because very clearly
– and it's not in the <u>spirit</u> of persecution to believe
this –

right now a cabal has been mounted against me and
which could have all kinds of repercussions.
This story of the Radio Broadcast is lamentable.
The texts may well appear in 'Combat' or as a book-
let
but you won't hear the sounds,
the sonorous xylophone passages,
the screams, the guttural noises and the voice,
all of which would have finally constituted a 1st ver-
sion of the Theatre of Cruelty.
It's a DISASTER for me.
Yours very sincerely,

Antonin Artaud.

Ivry-sur-Seine, 13 February 1948

Dear Marc Barbezat

I've now written to you on two occasions to ask you to send back to me the manuscript notebook containing the text
<u>Tutuguri</u>
dramatic poem concerning
<u>the Dance of the Sun</u>
of the Tarahumara Indians.
I've received nothing. So I am asking you yet again to send me back the manuscript notebook containing the text
<u>Tutuguri</u>
which I need with great urgency.
You are aware that <u>Tutuguri</u> forms part of a radio programme <u>which has been censored</u>.
Consequently, I've found a publisher who will publish the complete texts of the radio programme which include the Tutuguri that was inserted into the radio programme along with sound effects, voices and an entire xylophony. I will give you another text concerning the Dance of the Sun: a text that will be longer than the Tutuguri. So I'm waiting for your sending of Tutuguri.
Very warmly,

Antonin Artaud

P.S. I've sent you other manuscipts
in addition to <u>Tutuguri</u>
for the Arbalète magazine:

'To alienate the actor'
The Theatre and science.
So I'm going to have to take back <u>Tutuguri</u> from you and send you a text to replace it, but <u>above all, give me back right now the manuscript notebook</u> of Tutuguri.

17 February 1948

My very dear friends,

I believe that what overwhelmed and impassioned certain people such as Georges Braque in hearing the Radio Broadcast 'The judgement of god' is, above all, the part with the sound effects and xylophonic passages, along with the poem read by Roger Blin and the one read by Paule Thévenin. It's vital to avoid spoiling the effect of those xylophonic passages through the prevaricating, dialectic and long-winded text at the beginning. I sent you an express mail to indicate a number of cuts for you to make and which would leave only a few sentences at the beginning and the end of the 'Introduction'.

I urge you to make those cuts,
I urge you
– both of you –
to VERIFY that those cuts are strictly made.
Nothing must subsist in this Radio Broadcast
which is liable to disappoint,
to cause boredom,
or to exasperate
an avid public that has been seized by all of the innovation which the sound effects and xylophonic passages bring about,
and which not even the Balinese, Chinese, Japanese and Sinhalese theatres contain.
I'm therefore counting on both of you
to go ahead and make those cuts, because they have not been made and I shake your hands in friendship.

Antonin Artaud

Tuesday 24 February 1948.

Paule, I'm very sad and disheartened,
my body is hurting me, everywhere,
but above all I have the impression that people were
disappointed
by my radio broadcast.
Wherever <u>the machine</u> is
there's always the abyss and the void,
there exists a technical interference which deforms
and annihilates whatever you have created.
The poor opinions of M. and of A. are unjustified but
they must have had their point of departure in that
transition's weakening of my work,
that's why I'm never again going to get involved with
Radio,
and from now onwards will devote myself
exclusively
to theatre
that is, in the way I conceive it,
a theatre of blood,
a theatre at which, at every performance,
<u>corporeally</u>
something is gained
not just for the performer but also for whoever comes
to see the performance,
moreover,
you are not performing,
it's an action.
In reality the theatre is the <u>genesis</u> of creation.
That is going to happen.
I had a vision this afternoon – I saw all those who are
going to follow me and who still do not totally have
their bodies because pigs like those at the restaurant

last night are eating too much. There are those who eat too much and there are others who, like me, cannot eat any longer without <u>spitting</u>.
Yours,

Antonin Artaud.

Ivry-sur-Seine, 25 February 1948

Dear Mr Barbezat

I never gave
the theatre and science
to <u>Combat</u>.
I don't even have the original manuscript of it, which
is in the hands of Henriette Gomez, 5, rue du Cirque
If they have published it, it was without asking for
my authorisation.
I'm pillaged and robbed from every direction.
I'm leaving on 15 March for <u>Antibes</u> and I'm going
to live there
I will give you my address there
but can you send back to me, temporarily, the note-
book containing the manuscript text of <u>Tutuguri</u>
Warmly yours,

Antonin Artaud

P.S. <u>Combat</u> published Tutuguri
(still without saying anything to me)
but as for the 'theatre and science'
the text to which I'm attached above all others,
you must have been badly informed or else have mixed-
up the titles,
Combat has published nothing of mine other than
<u>Tutuguri</u>, and an extract from 'Van Gogh'
So I'll await from you the proofs of the two little books.

Antonin Artaud

P.S. Don't forget to bring me back the manuscript of
Tutuguri when you come here at the end of February –

I'll still be at Ivry then.

I am leaving for Antibes on 15 March. The journey is going to demand <u>huge</u> costs for moving-in there. See what you would be able to give me for that.

P.S. Above all, please don't forget the <u>money order</u> that I am asking you for, for my journey to the South. Thank you.

Dernière visite à
ANTONIN ARTAUD
poète foudroyé

Interview de Jean MARABINI

ANTONIN ARTAUD est mort hier matin à l'asile d'Ivry. A l'heure où l'on porte le bol de café au lait et le morceau de pain aux malades, l'infirmière de service découvrait le corps d'Antonin Artaud, allongé par terre et sans vie. Il avait dû tenter de se vêtir. Il tenait encore une chaussure à la main.

J'étais allé le voir la semaine dernière. Il m'avait confié qu'il était atteint du cancer et qu'il abschait de fortes doses de « chloral » pour apaiser ses souffrances. Il y a une quinzaine, il avait refusé une invitation de ses intimes qui voulaient l'emmener dans le Midi ; il leur avait dit : « Pas l'hiver, début mars je serai mort ». La prophétie s'est réalisée.

Il habitait une chambre desolée dans ce qui fut l'ancien pavillon de chasse d'un Orléans. Il n'allongeait pas d'une immense chambre sur un grabat. Au mur, des dessins fulgurants rappelaient les esquisses de Van Gogh.

Il me déclara une nuit d'hiver : « Jusqu'à quelle teinte du mois trois-cents ensemble ? » et sur l'édition de son « Van Gogh », il répond : « La teinte du sang trouvera le noir ». Il se leva, d'une main tremblante une cigarette, arpenta la large pièce :

— Je sais que j'ai le cancer. Ce que je veux dire avant de mourir, c'est que le bois les psychiatres. A Rodez, le vivre dans la terreur de celle grappe : à M. Artaud je mange pas aujourd'hui, il pense au Dieu... Je sais qu'il y a des tortures plus abominables, je pense à Van Gogh, à Nerval, à tous les autres. Ce qui me trouve, c'est qu'au XXe siècle un médecin puisse s'emparer d'un homme sous prétexte qu'il est fou et faire de lui ce qu'il lui plaît. J'ai subi cinquante et un électro-chocs...

Devant tout ceci, que reste-t-il de l'ancien Artaud ?
des notes
celles du puisatier qui monte sans soleil, hors de la voûte ronde.
barre à barre sur l'escalier du temps
gangrené par l'éternité.
Les voici, à travers un certain passé.

— Antonin ARTAUD.

(Fragments d'un poème inédit)

La semaine prochaine, suite de « Dernière Visite à... » Les critiques jugées par eux-mêmes... et par les autres.

COLLECTION
INCIDENCES
VIENT DE PARAÎTRE
SAINT-JUST
PAGES CHOISIES
Préface par JEAN CASSOU

FLAUBERT
BOUVARD et PÉCUCHET

ÉDITIONS DU POINT DU JOUR

VIENT DE PARAÎTRE
JACQUES FAURIE
ESSAI SUR LA SÉDUCTION
« L'Art d'aimer selon "Les Liaisons dangereuses" »
LA TABLE RONDE

Partage de Claude
par Justin SAGET

PORTRAIT DE MESA

LA BÊTE A-T-ELLE ÉTÉ
LES LIVRES, par Maurice N...

Le grand écrivain irlandais
LIAM O'FLAHERTY
qui vient de publier en traduction française : « Famine » et « L'Ile de la Colère »

Brève rencontre avec
Liam O'Flaherty
par Dominique ARBAN

IL fallait bien qu'il fût ainsi : de haute stature, de calme aisance, le visage de ce rouge sensible et délicat des types de Provence, et les yeux bleus ensoleillés. Un Irlandais. Moi, je me figurais autrement l'auteur du « Mouchard », du « Puritain », de « Famine » aussi, qui paraît aujourd'hui en France et qui raconte...

LE CAPITAINE PAUL
Grand roman d'aventures par Alexandre DUMAS

Résumé

Artaud's Final Interviews

Published in the Newspapers *Combat* and *Le Figaro Littéraire*

26/27 and 28 February 1948

These two newspaper interviews from the final week of Artaud's life – his last public words and acts, published on what are now yellowed, large-format newsprint media pages, alongside Cold War-era articles on such subjects as Soviet heavy industry and the new Marshall Plan's deliveries of US wheat to France – have never been republished. Artaud had previously given interviews from the mid 1920s to the mid 1930s, on his film-acting roles and his plans for 'Theatre of Cruelty' performances, but none between those previous interviews and these final two interviews. The interviews followed on from the censorship furore over Artaud's final radio work and the subsequent events – the last of which had taken place on 23 February 1948, three or four days before the *Combat* journalist's visit to Artaud in Ivry-sur-Seine – that had been organised with the aim to try to overturn that censorship. Both interviews were published shortly after Artaud's death; his voice in the interviews and its publication in the newspapers is traversed by death.

Combat and *Le Figaro* were prominent but dissimilar Parisian newspapers, each with large readerships. *Combat* originated in 1941 in clandestine resistance to France's German Occupation and still had the masthead 'From Resistance to Revolution'; it would cease publication in 1974. Artaud was actively engaged in his last years in attempting to have his work published in *Combat*, frequently sending its editors (such as Albert Camus) letters and new texts with demands to publish them in the newspaper. The conservative newspaper *Le Figaro* – still extant in 2023 – had been founded in 1826; *Le Figaro Littéraire* was a weekly literary supplement to the main newspaper, and was sold separately from it at the time of Artaud's interview.

Jean Marabini visited Artaud at his pavilion in Ivry-sur-Seine on either Thursday 26 or Friday 27 February, while Jean Desternes' visit took place on Saturday 28 February. Marabini was the better-known of the two: a 25-year-old, up-and-coming literary journalist who had met Artaud before. He would later publish several books on urban and political history, including a 1959 illustrated study of the Soviet Union in the filmmaker and editor Chris Marker's celebrated 'Petite Planète' book series, as well as a 1970 science-fiction novel, *Year 2021: The Insane Children*. Desternes, also a young journalist, specialised at that time in film and radio articles (and later in travel writing); he appears to have exasperated Artaud and to have been overawed by his visit to Artaud's pavilion. Both journalists asked Artaud few if any questions, and mainly confined themselves to transcribing what he said to them. Marabini partly narrates the interview in the present tense, giving it a strange immediacy. The location of the interviews – Artaud's pavilion – is vividly evoked by Marabini as a sombre, haunting building engulfed within the surrounding fir trees, and occupied by a man awaiting but adamantly refusing death. Marabini appears to locate the pavilion within the grounds of an insane asylum rather than (as was really the case) a dilapidated convalescence home whose occupants or their families paid monthly sums for their stays there. In contrast to Marabini's death-inflected perception of Artaud's pavilion and the wooded garden hiding it, Artaud's friends such as Paule Thévenin and Jacques Prevel remembered that location as being uniquely ideal and sustaining for Artaud's last work, evoking the pavilion and the parkland as being edenic, silent and outside of time, despite their close proximity to one of Ivry-sur-Seine's main avenues. Artaud died in his pavilion on the night of 3–4 March 1948, a few days after Desternes' visit.

These interviews were translated directly from original copies of the two newspapers from 1948 held at the Bibliothèque nationale de France.

LAST VISIT TO ANTONIN ARTAUD, THE POET STRUCK BY LIGHTNING

INTERVIEW BY JEAN MARABINI,
PUBLISHED IN *COMBAT*, 5 MARCH 1948.

MARABINI'S INTERVIEW WITH ARTAUD ALSO
APPEARED IN THE ARTS JOURNAL *OPÉRA* ON
10 MARCH 1948.

Antonin Artaud died yesterday morning at the asylum of Ivry. At the early hour when bowls of coffee with milk and pieces of bread are brought to the inmates, the nurse on duty discovered the body of Antonin Artaud, stretched out on the ground and lifeless. He must have been in the act of getting dressed. He still held a shoe in one of his hands.

Last week, I went to see him. He confided in me that he had cancer and was swallowing down large doses of 'chloral' to alleviate his sufferings. Two weeks or so ago, he had refused the invitation of close friends who had wanted to take him down to the South Coast. He had told them: 'End of February, beginning of March, I'm going to be dead.' That prophecy was accurate.

He was living in a desolate room in what had once been one of the dukes of Orléans' hunting pavilions. Next to an immense fireplace, he was stretched out on a rickety old bed. On the walls were his searing drawings, which reminded me of Van Gogh's sketches.

He writes a dedication for me on a photograph of himself: 'Into which stain of blood are we going to travel together?', and on a copy of his book on Van Gogh he writes the response: 'The stain of blood will touch the darkness.' He stands up, lights up a Gauloise with a trembling hand, then walks rapidly around the large room:

– I know that I have cancer. What I want to say before dying is: that I hate psychiatrists. At Rodez, I lived in terror of hearing this sentence: 'Mr Artaud isn't eating today – let's give him an electroshock.' I know that there are still more heinous tortures. I'm thinking of Van Gogh, of Nerval, of all the others. What is most atrocious, is that in the 20th century a doctor is able to seize hold of someone on the pretext that they're mad and do with them whatever he likes. I endured fifty sessions of electroshock, which means I endured fifty comas. For a long time, I was in a state of amnesia. I had even forgotten my friends: Marthe Robert, Henri Thomas, Adamov. I no longer recognised Jean-Louis Barrault. The only doctor who ever did me any good was Dr Delmas, here, at Ivry, and sadly, he's now dead...'.

He continues, in a feverish voice:

– I am disgusted with psychoanalysis, with this 'freudism' that defiles everything. I want now to conceive solely of purity. All those who have left behind something of themselves – Edgar Allan Poe, Baudelaire, Van Gogh – were the chaste ones. I can only create something myself when I'm chaste.

– *'From what you're saying, I could believe that you're a Christian.'*

– All that has got nothing to do with God. I talked about that in my notorious radio broadcast that went awry. And moreover – I had nothing at all to do with any of the scandal that has been made of it... Religion always equivocated on these questions. Not me: on the contrary, I believe we must have done with the sexual human being.

– What I'm telling you is that we have lost a particular conception of the human being. Around the year 1,000, nobody died. There was an era when people lived for several centuries. Entire villages of the living dead existed at that time, as they still exist now in certain remote locations in Asia.

– For as long as philosophers are going to believe that there is, on the one hand, the mind, and on the other hand, the body: the world isn't going to move forward. All that counts is the human body, which is lost as soon as it thinks. In that former time, the act was direct: no kind of mental debate existed; the hand never disputed with itself whether to seize something or else not to seize it.

– Right now, I want to destroy my thought and my mind. Above all, to destroy thought, mind and consciousness; I don't want to suppose anything, admit anything, enter into anything, discuss anything...

A long silence interrupted only by the crackling of the fire's logs. Now I remember that, one day, he had confided to me that, in 'chloral', he had discovered that freedom for which he was searching, and a kind of deliverance from his obsessions: what he called his 'internal spinning'. Now, next to the hearth, I can see the iron bar which he broke clean in two during his last nocturnal delirium. He was, on that occasion, animated by a force that was infernal.

Outside, the fir trees: a lost pavilion hidden in undergrowth. He tells me this building is the Mortuary and that this outlandish undergrowth which surrounds it – only two hundred metres on one side from a forest, two hundred metres on the other side from factory chimneys – could well be the 'Garden of death' of Hans Christian Andersen.

Antonin Artaud has been contemplating his end for weeks. That freedom he was searching desperately for: he has now finally found it.

(Fragments of an unpublished poem):

In face of all that, what remains of the old Artaud?

some notes

those of the excavator who is rising up sunless,
     beyond the round vault,

bar by bar on the staircase of time

made gangrenous by eternity.

There they are, through a certain past time.

Antonin ARTAUD.

LAST VISIT TO ANTONIN ARTAUD

INTERVIEW BY JEAN DESTERNES,
PUBLISHED IN *LE FIGARO LITTÉRAIRE*,
13 MARCH 1948.

On a grey morning: Ivry. A wedding party is coming down from the old church stuck up on the 'Monument to the Dead' hillside. In a blue mist, the procession disappears behind the huts of the fairground, the bride lifting her dress's train above the mud.

It's Saturday morning. For the first and last time, I am going to meet Antonin Artaud, four days before his death, alone, in a bare room, deep within a garden.

I hammer at the window. Knotted fingers pull up the blind and the mask of Artaud stares at me through the glass.

– What is it!

He's holding his head inclined on his hand, and the enormous forehead tilts forward like a helmet made of frail skin. Everything, in that face, appears to throb, the two swollen veins on the temples, the black wings of long hair, the pinched nose. He opens the door to me, a little taken aback.

He apologises for the squalid state of his room, with a gesture of weariness which sweeps across the dirt-encrusted walls, the stains of damp, the desolate void surrounding the bed which takes central place in the room.

An icy sweat drenches me when – in a ragged voice of sudden bursts, with tragic stammerings like sobs – he explains to me how he has known and touched death:

– Yes, I've seen the hideous face of Death. When I was at the asylum of Rodez, I fell into the abyss. When I entered the office of Dr Ferdière and asked him for twenty-five drops of laudanum – because I was suffering atrociously with my stomach, and piercing pains were sawing away at my back – he replied to me: 'Not only I am not going to give you your twenty-five drops, but now I'm also going to cure you of your desire to have them, by subjecting you to electroshocks.'*

– Yes, I was in Death's waiting-room. It's claimed by some that you remember nothing of electroshocks. But not me: I say: 'I remember'.

– I was aware – I was perfectly aware – of horrendous visions that I was able to attribute without any possible error to those black and bottomless pits, to that artificial coma. Visions that were infinitely painful, and which fled from me whenever I tried to scrape them away intact from that terrifying magma. Visions that I cannot describe now, because they have become submerged into the uncertain, and there is nothing I detest so much as imprecision, as the glueing of that agony into the beyond. And I plunged into Death. I know what Death is.

Someone brings him his lunch, and I want to get out of there, but he insists that I should stay. Even so, I'm horribly troubled. He asks my permission to eat in front of him, and very rapidly swallows great mouthfuls of noodles, bent-up askew on his bed, on which he's placed his plate. Then he searches for his drawings for 'Artaud the Mômo', but doesn't find them, then he continues to eat, while explaining to me – in his muffled voice – that he was once locked up, naked under his shirt, in a cell, on a straw mattress positioned directly on the ground.

– And for years, they replied to whoever came to try to find out what was happening to me: 'Antonin Artaud is dead!'

He repeats that sentence several times over, with a frozen expression of contempt. Then he dips a corner of his napkin into a blue jug of water, rubs both sides of his nose so that a red stain spreads out across the centre of his blanched face, and takes the empty plates over to the door. An acrid smoke is stinging our eyes.

– This fire is the only luxury I have here, the only magnificent element of this room.

He abruptly leans back in his armchair and rubs the area below his ribcage, on both sides, for a long time, then seizes a great iron bar which he uses to chop up the fire's logs.

– It was with an iron bar like this one that an agent of the Police Force broke my vertebral column, one day, in Ireland, when I was calmly walking while carrying a cane that had been identified with the stick of Saint Patrick. And it's from that day that the terrible tortures began – those tortures that psychiatrists claim are the results of hallucinations…

I ask him if his health is better now.

– But I've never – never – been mentally ill. I was locked up because I wanted to defend myself against people who were intending to assault me in the cabin of a boat, while I was just looking at the sea through the porthole. One of them threatened me with an enormous wrench while the other was screaming out for him to strike me. I threw the table at them and I was placed in a straitjacket... But I've never been affected in my mental life. Physically, yes: I've always been a detritus.

A young woman arrives and speaks to him with great gentleness. Artaud appears transformed when she proposes plans for outings. He suggests that we take a short walk in the garden. Facing his door, there's the bust of a Roman emperor.

– For two years now, he's been staring at me ceaselessly. Just take a look at that. That's sinister!

With a gesture, he indicates to us his little pavilion with its slate roof.

– I've been told about horrible things which went on in that room. It's there *(he points out the belltowers of the town hall visible above the little wall)* that in 1789, for the first time, the cry 'No god, no master!' was heard. One of the king's guardsmen wanted to stop that. He was taken off to the room where I'm living, to be butchered. That's not all: Gérard de Nerval lived there for some time.

The young woman re-enters the room first. She stokes the fire.

– No, no – not in the shape of a cross. Never put the logs crossways!

– Please excuse me, Antonin Artaud, I wasn't thinking...

He pulls apart the bedclothes and stretches out, then takes a look at the sketch that he's outlined on a sheet of paper fixed to the wall with four drawing-pins. It seems to be someone being tortured, someone skinned

alive, confined in the web of his nerves.
To some question or other, he cries out:

– To get out of this, I know only one way!

He takes a knife from his pocket, opens it up slowly and then, with a sudden strike, embeds it into the table which already displays the evidence of previous attacks of that kind.

– That's the only means to get out of it – the knife – yes, that's the only weapon to use against those bastards. Their crime: that is what is not being considered enough. You have got to act now – and not to chatter, to debate idiotically as you and I are doing at this moment. *Elsewhere*, yes, elsewhere, there are people who are engaged in acts, or who are getting ready to commit acts. People who are going to band together. And it's not going to be like the uprising of Petrograd or of Moscow. This will be very greatly more terrible and more vast...

He is gently humming to himself, stroking his ears, his elbows raised up.

– I am haunted – *haun-ted* for a long time now – by a kind of writing which is not within the norm. I've wanted to write outside of grammar, to find a means of expression beyond words. And now and then I've believed myself to be very close, to that kind of expression... but everything is driving me back to the norm.

I had the impression that he already belonged to another world. And when I'd got back to the métro station, in that dirty end of winter glow, I couldn't shake off my icy stupour. But I knew very well that I would eventually be able to dispel the weight of that solitude and unease, while, for Artaud, it would be unending anguish – penetrating anguish, as he called it – for as long as he would still have to bear the burden of living, this 'anguish in bursts, punctuated by voids, tightened and pressed together like nails'.

Until that night when Death – that presence familiar to his internal struggle – had to arrive to give him deliverance.

* [note: Dr Gaston Ferdière (1907–90) was the director of the Rodez asylum during the three years Artaud spent there (1943–46); he instigated Artaud's electro-convulsive therapy, which he viewed as innovative and beneficial, but usually delegated the treatment's application (51 documented sessions in all) to his assistants. He and Artaud remained in intermittent contact by letter during Artaud's time in Ivry-sur-Seine, in part because Artaud needed Ferdière to send manuscripts which had been left behind at Rodez to his new publishers, such as Marc Barbezat; Ferdière also attended the second of the reading events that marked Artaud's exhibition of his drawings at the Galerie Pierre in Paris in July 1947, though Ferdière received hostile reactions there from Artaud's friends, and Artaud himself increasingly denounced him in 1946–48 with a raw severity that Ferdière often told me, in interviews across the second half of the 1980s, still wounded him and often made him weep. Artaud's statement in this interview is his last word on Ferdière. After the Rodez asylum's closure, Ferdière had a long, itinerant career in many hospitals and clinics in France, while also participating in the promotion of the art brut/outsider art movement. During the 1960s, in Paris, he treated artists and writers such as Hans Bellmer, Unica Zürn and Isidore Isou. At the end of his life, while writing poetry which he told me was 'too obscene to be published', he lived in a riverside house in Héricy, south of Paris.]

L'opération
du
magasin
terré

ARTAUD'S
LAST NOTEBOOK

THE FIRST DAYS OF MARCH 1948

Artaud's hundreds of pierced, stained and assailed notebooks from the years 1945–48, from Rodez and then Ivry-sur-Seine, are archived together in drawers on one side of the Bibliothèque nationale de France's manuscript reading-room. There is some kind of exceptional ritual at stake whenever the archivists are asked to bring out the last notebook of all, from the drawers' extreme end, as though its green cover held or embodied some kind of forensic evidence from which the residues of Artaud's death – an act of diabolical, magical or social assassination, or an amalgam of all three, for him – can be investigated and exposed.

The final notebook's contents have been translated directly from the pages of the original notebook itself (an inexpensive schoolchildren's notebook, as with all of the others), with the support of Guillaume Fau. The arrangement of the notebook pages, inscribed in green ink and in pencil, accords with the printed pages here; two pages are devoted entirely to drawings. The notebook holds glossolalia, simply transcribed here. Only the first twenty-two pages were used, before its abrupt curtailing at the instant of Artaud's death on the night of 3–4 March 1948.

During twelve months from the autumn of 2006, to autumn 2007, in that high-ceilinged, often-sunlit manuscripts room of the Bibliothèque nationale de France, I read all of Artaud's hundreds of notebooks from the asylum of Rodez and then from his time at his Ivry-sur-Seine pavilion, one after the other (apart from the very few that are missing, having been stolen, or which have slipped into private collections). On winter days, unless I was hallucinating it, some of the notebooks – once their pages had been opened – still gave off a compacted smell of cigarette and wood smoke, coal, damp, invoking the Paris streets and cafes of 1948, or the interior of the Ivry-sur-Seine pavilion, even the smell of Artaud's coat-pockets' interiors, or his body...

Notebook 406

[Written on the notebook's cover:]

**The execration
of
the <u>inborn</u>
magician**

[the first page]

You, you've asked me
nothing
and nobody, on this subject matter,
has
    ever asked me anything
(everybody sticks to their
own thing,
    knowing all too well
    without any doubt
what they need to hang on to)

so I'll say this
    yes
<u>magic exists</u>

And you may well not even know
to what extent
    it has always existed.
It exists just as the
vault of the nocturnal
firmament exists,
as a rosary's
unending succession of beads exists,

because, far more so than
religion itself,
magic has always existed.

    Here and there
religion
is the putting into practice
of an archaic ritual that is now more
or less
    lapsed
but magic,
    that
is a fact,
a sinister one, perhaps,
    but a fact.

Without any ceremonial,
or any ritual,
without any practices
of theurgy
    that have become frozen
magic exists as though it were

[the third page]

the sweeping wind of a fact
    which has never stopped
    wiping out everything

        fantaï
        at noch
        and
        maï
        now hardened

        orak
        akompf
        akompf
        <u>pfünchë</u>

[the fourth page is unused]

[the fifth page]

omono
    zet
    o
kano
zi   the sonic tissue
    of the radio broadcast

    Thursday 4 March
      1948
11 30 in the morning, Bernard Amouroux.*

* [note: Bernard Amouroux was an editor of the K publishing com-
pany that was preparing in March 1948 to publish a book of the
censored texts of Artaud's radio broadcast, *To have done with
the judgement of god*. On the morning of 4 March 1948, he arrived
for his appointment at Artaud's pavilion in Ivry-sur-Seine not long
after Artaud had been found dead there by the clinic's staff.]

[the sixth page]

on the
mountains' slopes of
Fortinbras
those of Norway
those of the world

The question
    that
    counts
    is that of
    of
    the I
    in movement
    to you
while passing through the arcades
over their main beams'
intercrossings.

[the eighth page holds drawings without texts]

[the ninth page holds drawings with a text]

Which
     will no
   longer exist
soon

[the tenth page holds drawings without texts]

[the eleventh page]

two fingers up against the forehead
    (the forefinger and the middle finger)
two fingers against the
    chest
the middle finger and the forefinger
comprise <u>the action</u> able to push away
    the evil of those
    low-down agitators

and I'm going to be remembering that

as for the sign that I'm
going to accomplish in order to recog
nise myself for myself,
that's never had anything to do with anyone
except myself
because beyond the rare individuals that I've
chosen – because I myself
made them – I am the universal enemy
of all men
having, moreover, spiked all of them down.

Magic
    low-down operating magic that
    works to dismantle the body's masonry
    and to propel it downwards,
    exists

(in the mind, that's what it says,
and in principle
<u>but never as a fact</u>)

magic which melts
the body down into a mind and
into a principle
which makes of the body
this spurt of
baby's whey,
this dripping of milk
that is isolated somewhere within
    the entire body's
    movement
    within the gait of
its entire masonry,

koundiar
koundiar
   o
neter
sor
païre
koundiar
   o
neter
se

[the fourteenth page is unused]

[the fifteenth page]

and I was waking up
    <u>propelled low-down</u>
with the <u>criminals</u>

– through the lowest jealousy
through hatred
    and through desire –

who activated
evil 100 times over with
with a greater and greater degree
of consciousness
and of science

who undertook that with a
consciousness
and
a science
that were more
    and more
    <u>refined</u>

[the sixteenth page]

god is going to be
 blown into oblivion
 by
an act of disintegration
 exerted in
 collaboration
 with
 my right
 ear
 and
 all that it holds
 by way of
 putrefaction

And along with that
all the
forces of the heavens
can come hurtle down
upon me;
since I know – know too much –
about the hole
– anal or vaginal –
through which they emerged:

<u>you're going to see it</u>

the
     an
        ger
that they believed
they'd extinguished
through pain,

that slow-moving
nutriti [note: this incomplete word is barred out]
nu
    tr
      it
        ion
           al
    silencing pain
    that belongs
    to time
it's still <u>there</u>
like a flame
of
cholera

    fortobengardu
fordabantagna [note: this word is barred out]
    koran
       ko
koranko   hartu [note: the first word in this line is barred out]
totarankegno
totarankhe
    kotarengarda
       ta   koranka

in order
    h'love
    (blood-soul
    blood

[the twentieth page]

blood

that will work

gold
    hasn't
        covered up
           the blood
you reverend gentlemen
    of Rome
    and
    of
       <u>Lhasa</u>

And they've made me
plummet
    into
    death
there, where I'm ceaselessly
eating
    cock
the anus too
    and
    shit
for all of my meals,
all those of <u>the cross</u> [note: this word is inscribed verti-
    cally, at the page's left margin:] Pulartilisation.

so, the same figure
returns every
morning (he is an other)
in order to accomplish his
    revolting, criminal
    and murderous, sinister
    mission   which is to
    maintain
the state of <u>bewitchment</u> cast upon
me

and to continue to
make of me
this eternally
bewitched man
        etc etc

GLOSSOLALIA

THE PROJECTION OF THE TRUE BODY, 1946–48

Artaud inscribed sequences of glossolalia around all four edges of *The Projection of the true body*, the most extraordinary of all of the fifty or so drawings he made while at Ivry-sur-Seine, in addition to many hundreds of drawings made in his notebooks. Most of Artaud's drawings from May 1946 to March 1948 were undertaken at his Ivry pavilion; occasionally, he made drawings in the apartments of his friends in central Paris and Charenton.

The Projection of the true body is unique in its execution having spanned more than a year of Artaud's time at Ivry-sur-Seine. He undertook the drawing six months after arriving there from Rodez, and signed and dated it, on 18 November 1946, but then reworked it and completed it in either January or February 1948. Throughout that interval, it was pinned to one of his pavilion's inner walls. The figure on the drawing's right-hand side could be Artaud's sinister 'assassin', or more likely, from the drawing's title, Artaud's projection of the authentic, organ-less body he envisioned for himself after passing through the corporeal transmutations, activated by feral 'wrong-way-round' dance, announced in *To have done with the judgement of god*'s final text.

Artaud's glossolalia form an exploratory corporeal language of fragmentation – far beyond national languages, and even further beyond translation – as well as a combative instrument to be incanted aloud against Artaud's assailants. They are a 'speaking in tongues' in which the tongue itself has already been excised from the body, leaving behind only raw skeletal fire that propels sound, or else screams, as with Artaud's recorded screams of 16 January 1948 in *To have done with the judgement of god*.

I transcribed the glossolaliac elements directly from the drawing itself, with Paule Thévenin's help; the overlayered glossolalia in pencil and black crayon were only disernible up-close, with a magnifying glass, but then became easily readable.

GLOSSOLALIA

THE PROJECTION OF THE TRUE BODY

[at the upper edge of the drawing:]

tarabut rabut karviston rabut rabut kur a vitctron.

[along the left border of the drawing: two texts, one inscribed on top of the other:]

kro
cm
krem
krem

ko
mar
da
var
ker
nim
nenti
nizam
taber
kembish.

[along the right border of the drawing:]

kra
nam
terzi
brou
mish

ter
ni
o nam
dermi
toman.

[along the drawing's lower edge: two texts, one inscribed over
the other:]

tarabut rabut karvizon rabut
rabut kar a viton
ger mat tarta karvilon
soarvila kortri la.

tarabut rabut karvizon
rabat karvizon
a ut karazon
krubat korozon a ra vi lernti

[inscribed alongside the drawing of Artaud's head:]

en.

AUX QUATRE VENTS

L'enterrement d'Antonin Artaud

ANTONIN ARTAUD a été enterré sans discours par ses compagnons de tous les jours.

Les photographes vinrent trop tard et manquèrent le convoi dans le parc de l'asile. Ils ne le rattrapèrent qu'au cimetière, la brève cérémonie terminée. On estima généralement que c'était fort bien ainsi.

Les premiers arrivés revirent encore une fois le masque net et ravagé : le corps d'Antonin Artaud fut mis en bière au tout dernier moment.

À dix heures trente, le cortège quittait la maison de santé pour l'un des quatre cimetières d'Ivry. On reconnaissait, derrière le corbillard, Jean Paulhan, Raymond Queneau, Adrienne Monnier, Henri Thomas, le metteur en scène Jean Vilar, les acteurs Roger Blin et Alain Cuny, Marthe Robert, les yeux rouges, soutenue par le fidèle Arthur Adamov.

Des petits groupes silencieux descendirent ensuite la colline, vers le métro.

L'enterrement civil n'avait pas duré une heure.

Antonin Artaud was buried, without any speeches, by his closest friends.

The photographers arrived too late and missed the funeral procession in the asylum park. They only caught up with it at the cemetery, once the short ceremony was already over. Everyone who attended thought that it was better that way.

The people who arrived first saw for the last time that sharp and ravaged mask: the body of Antonin Artaud was placed in his coffin only at the very last moment.

At ten thirty in the morning [8 March 1948], the procession left the convalescence home for one of Ivry's four cemeteries. Behind the hearse, the familiar figures could be seen of Jean Paulhan, Raymond Queneau, Adrienne Monnier, Henri Thomas, the director Jean Vilar, the actors Roger Blin and Alain Cuny, Marthe Robert, with reddened eyes, supported by Artaud's friend Arthur Adamov.

The silent small groups then descended the hill, towards the métro station.

The non-religious ceremony had lasted less than an hour.

'Antonin Artaud's burial', an anonymous report in *Le Figaro Littéraire*, Paris, 13 March 1948.

CONTENTS

© DIAPHANES 2023
ISBN 978-3-0358-0356-3
All rights reserved

Hardcover edition published by
Infinity Land Press, London, 2022

DIAPHANES
Limmatstrasse 270 | CH-8005 Zurich
Dresdener Str. 118 | D-10999 Berlin
57 Rue de la Roquette | F-75011 Paris

Printed in Germany
Layout: 2edit, Zurich

www.diaphanes.net